PEACEMAKER
FOR HIRE

PEACEMAKER
FOR HIRE

•

CLIFFORD BLAIR

AVALON BOOKS
THOMAS BOUREGY AND COMPANY, INC.
401 LAFAYETTE STREET
NEW YORK, NEW YORK 10003

PRINTED IN THE UNITED STATES OF AMERICA
ON ACID-FREE PAPER
BY HADDON CRAFTSMEN, SCRANTON, PENNSYLVANIA

To Boyd Rayburn

Friend, pastor, spiritual mentor, and fellow fan
of good old-fashioned Westerns

Prologue

James Stark knew they were waiting for him. He had
ridden the manhunter's trail too long not to be able to
read the signs when the quarry had decided to turn on
the hunter.

He had read it in the curious meanderings of the tracks
of the four owlhoots over the past few miles. They were
no longer pushing their horses straight ahead in an attempt to put as much distance as possible between them
and their pursuer. Rather, they were straying close to the
rocky hills and wooded draws that marred the rolling
grassland here and there. They were straying close, and
then riding on, like men looking for something . . . looking for a likely spot to set up an ambush for the lone
wolf who had trailed them so relentlessly over the past
days.

Stark had read it too, in the contours of the rugged
bluff up ahead. Raw outcroppings of rock and deep gullies cut by rainwater scarred the red soil of its surface.

1

A sorry thicket of blackjack oak and a tangle of under-brush had managed to survive on the traces of moisture left by the runoff water. There were a half-dozen likely spots overlooking the prairie where a bushwhacker might hole up and wait for his target.

And, finally, he read it in the slight feral lifting of his hackles as he eyed that drygulcher's terrain.

Stark's big sorrel stallion snorted impatiently. Stark drew the reins taut, holding the horse just within the fringe of woods clinging to the shallow creek he had crossed. The hombres lying in wait for him couldn't see him until he emerged from cover. Once out in the open, he would be under their guns for a good seventy-five yards of ground.

He glanced up through the leafy interlaced branches, gauging the whereabouts of the sun in the cloud-flecked sky. Most of the afternoon still lay before him, he cal-culated. The owlhoots couldn't be sure how far back he was. And they likely had gotten fed up enough with him dogging their trail that they'd be willing to wait a good long spell for him to ride into their sights.

He had been after them for nigh onto a week now. His standing retainer paid by the fledgling Oklahoma Territory Bankers Association had set him on the tracks of the outlaws from his Guthrie office when the four of them had hit the small bank in the town of Meridian to the tune of several thousand dollars. For the hefty fees they paid him, the Association expected—and got—fast action when member banks fell prey to the scourge of stickup artists and desperadoes plaguing Oklahoma Ter-ritory.

True, the U.S. Marshal's Office, headed by the re-doubtable Evett Nix, did yeoman's work in trying to corral the lawlessness rife in the area. The ranks of the deputies reporting to Nix boasted such legendary star-packers as Heck Thomas, Bill Tilghman, and Chris Madsen, who had all seen action in the wide-open West of the old days.

But their jurisdiction halted at Hell's Fringe, the boundary line between Oklahoma Territory and the Indian Lands, and it was across this boundary line that the bank robbers had fled, well in front of the posse that had been dispatched after them. The Lands were a haven for such men, a virtually lawless realm where the fastest six-gun wrote the statutes, and the best-aimed bullet enforced them.

The tribal police had authority over disputes within the various tribes that had been forcibly relocated there as the expanding mass of white men pushed them inexorably from their traditional lands. But the tribal lawmen could do little against the flood of owlhoots, desperadoes, stickup artists, hard cases, and gunslicks who had drifted or fled into the Lands when things got too hot for them in other parts of the shrinking West. Nor was the U.S. Cavalry likely to take a hand in such matters.

Thus it was that the bankers and certain other groups found it good business to have James Stark on retainer, ready to step into the breach and protect their interests when the minions of official law enforcement were hogtied by the very laws they served.

Acting as an independent private operative, Stark was free to cross over Hell's Fringe into the Indian Lands on missions such as this one, which had brought him to the edge of the woods, gazing suspiciously to where he suspected ruthless men lay in wait for his blood.

But he could play at this deadly game of ambush as well. If his hunch and his instincts were wrong, which he doubted, he would only be out a little time. If they were right, then, Lord willing, he could bring this chase to an end before the day was out.

"Easy, Red," he murmured to the sorrel as the animal tossed its head again.

Something in his voice quieted the horse, made it prick its ears back expectantly. He had covered a lot of miles on the trail of lawbreakers while astride the sorrel. Maybe Red could sense the taut wariness in his tones.

Carefully he worked the horse back away from the edge of the woods, then turned him along the course of the creekbed. They were protected from view on the bluff by the screen of trees and undergrowth. Red stepped delicately among the dead leaves and fallen branches, making surprisingly little noise for all his size. Yeah, the big horse knew they were being hunted too.

Automatically Stark eased the old Colt .45 Peacemaker revolver in its worn holster. His trademark, he had heard it called, and he had taken it as the symbol and name of his business enterprise. It had been with him for a spell longer than even the faithful Red.

He touched the hilt of the custom bowie knife in its sheath, and ran his hand over the butt of the Winchester lever-action shotgun riding in the saddle scabbard. Finally, he reached behind him to check the little Marlin double-action .38 nestled snugly in the concealed holster on the inside of his gunbelt.

Tools of his trade, he mused. He figured he'd be putting them to use before too much longer.

He stayed with the creekbed until he was past the bluff, then paused to survey the formation from his new vantage point. After a moment he brought out his fine German-made field glasses and scanned the uneven surface of the bluff. Details sprang into startling clarity: draws and gullies choked with underbrush, bare red earth, even a lazy rattler sunning its sinuous five-foot length on a flat slab of sandstone. The owlhoots weren't the only killers lurking in that rugged terrain. He'd need to step mighty careful.

Satisfied at last that his quarry wasn't concealed on this end of the rocky hill, he replaced the glasses in his saddlebag. Red rolled a watchful eye back at him as he stepped down out of the hull and lifted the shotgun from its scabbard.

"Don't go wandering off, fellow." He ran a palm down the sleekly muscled neck. Well trained, the sorrel would wait for him. He hoped the wait wouldn't be a permanent one. . . .

He gauged the stretch of open ground between his position and the base of the escarpment. Some cover was there for a man who knew how to use it.

Stark shucked his boots and donned his high Apache moccasins. Such footgear had helped make the old Indian warriors masters of silence and stealth.

Staying low, at times going to his belly, he dodged and darted and crept across the open terrain, relying on the tall grass and low swells of the ground for concealment. At the base of the bluff he paused in its shadow. No one had fired at him; his probing eyes could detect no signs of life. The basking rattler was out of his range of vision.

His moccasined feet were soundless as he headed up the grade, moving from rock to rock, snaking along the bare ground or following the courses of convenient gullies. He was careful not to raise any betraying dust, or to let any of his weapons clatter against stone.

He avoided the area where he'd seen the rattlesnake, but once a scorpion the size of his palm scuttled from under his descending hand. Tight-lipped, he watched it disappear into a crevice.

Frequently, as he climbed, he paused to study the terrain through narrowed eyes and test the breeze with flaring nostrils. The scent of an hombre who'd been hugging horseflesh hard for a handful of days without stopping to take a bath could carry a goodly distance to a trained set of nostrils.

He was working for the high ground, hoping to get above and behind his prey, but he could only guess as to their probable location, and take care not to stumble unexpectedly upon them. A growing urgency prodded him. The owlhoots could've been waiting for some time now, and might be losing patience. It was possible they'd give up their vigil and pull out before he had a chance to spot them. But he couldn't afford to let haste make him careless.

He halted in a crouch behind a blocky boulder and tested the breeze once more. A scent it carried made him bare his teeth in grim satisfaction. Tobacco smoke. Somewhere, not far ahead of him, some hombre had fired up a quirley, probably bored with waiting for a victim who wasn't obliging enough to ride into his sights.

Stark peered around the boulder. He still couldn't spot anyone, but a gully cut by rainwater snaked its way down at an angle in the direction he wanted to go. Leaving the shelter of the boulder, he slipped into the gully. It was deep enough so that he only had to crouch slightly to keep under cover.

With probing fingers he checked the barrel of the shotgun to be sure it hadn't gotten plugged with dirt or pebbles in all his crawling about.

First issued by Winchester only a few years back in 1887, the ten-gauge, lever-action repeating shotgun had proven itself a worthwhile addition to his personal weaponry. Its thirty-two-inch barrel gave it a respectable range, and the stopping power packed into the four shells in its magazine more than made up, in Stark's mind, for the greater number of shots possible with the more common repeating rifles. He alternated .00 buckshot with solid lead slugs in the loads he used, and he carried additional shells in the bandolier strapped across his chest.

The barrel was clear. Stark nodded with satisfaction and eased forward down the draw. He froze as a man's voice spoke in bored tones.

"Shoot, he ain't coming. I misdoubt there was anyone there anyway!"

"He was back there, all right," another voice rejoined. "Who do you think that was Buck saw when he doubled back yesterday?"

"Likely just some pilgrim riding the same trail we was. Sure wasn't the Peacemaker, like he thought; I'll say that!"

A disgusted mutter answered him.

Stark inched along the gully until he calculated he was some fifteen feet behind their position. Sounded to be just the two of them. Their pards must've kept on riding. This pair would have their attention fixed on the trail below, not on the draw at their backs.

Gingerly, using his hand to muffle the sound, he levered the shotgun, putting a load of buckshot under the cocked hammer. Doffing his Stetson, he lifted his head to peer over the rim of the gully.

He hadn't been far off in his calculations. About five yards distant, two ragged-looking men were hunkered down behind a screen of brush that, Stark guessed, overlooked the route he had been riding. One of them was just settling back from taking a look down the trail. The other was drawing on the cigarette that had betrayed them. Both were clad in well-worn range clothes and were packing sidearms. Their rifles were close at hand beside them.

Stark crouched back out of sight. He sleeved sweat from his forehead and clamped his Stetson back on his head. Then he raised up just enough to bring the barrel of the shotgun over the edge of the gully and center it midway between the pair.

"Wait's over, boys," he drawled. "Sorry I'm late."

Both gunslicks stiffened. The cigarette was motionless in the smoker's fingers. His compadre edged a hand toward his rifle.

"You're covered," Stark advised coolly. "Load of double-ought. Either of you makes a play, and you've both bought it."

The creeping hand halted.

"Lift them," Stark ordered.

Grudgingly the pair elevated their hands. The smoker still held his quirley forgotten in his hand. The smoke rising from it wavered tremulously in the air. The other one cranked his head around a notch at a time for a look-see.

Now that he'd eliminated the danger of either of them pulling a fast one, Stark straightened the rest of the way, letting the curious one get a good look at him.

The yahoo's stubbled face paled. "It is him!" he spat angrily. "The Peacemaker himself!"

His pard let out a stifled oath and dropped the cigarette, which had finally burned down to his fingers. Beyond that, he didn't move.

"Shuck your irons and turn around. Move real slow while you're doing it."

Again the obedience was reluctant. Two six-guns hit the dirt, and the pair pivoted slowly about. The smoker stared at Stark, then looked past him. His lips twisted upward in a cold grin of satisfaction.

That grin was all wrong, Stark knew with sudden instinctive savvy. It told him that maybe the other two owlhoots hadn't ridden on ahead after all. Maybe they had figured he'd turn the tables on their pards, and had waited around to try to return the favor. The familiar click of a gun coming to full cock was the only other warning he had.

Stark flung himself down to the floor of the gully as a hail of gunfire from behind rent the air above him. He felt his old Stetson snatched from his head, and heard one of the pair in front of him let out a startled cry.

He scrambled several feet down the gully as the gunfire tapered to a halt. Some remote part of his mind registered automatically that at least one six-shooter and a goodly portion of a repeater's magazine had been emptied at him. He squirmed over onto his shoulders, shotgun angled back the way he had come, and tried to still the ragged tear of his breath in his throat.

"Did we get him?" a gruff voice demanded in the silence of the gunfire's aftermath.

"You bet! Didn't you see his hat go flying? I drilled him plumb through the skull!"

"Hey, Buck!" called one of the first pair of bushwhackers. "You done hit Jake with all that shooting! He's down!"

"Shut up!" snarled the boaster. "Just stay put while we check on things. You reloaded yet, Rio?"

"Yep," the other drygulcher replied. "He went down right there in front of us. Be ready to plug him again if he moves."

Stark heard the scuffling of their approaching footsteps. A cold determination settled over him with almost comfortable familiarity, dissolving the tension that twisted in his gut. In its place was only a driving will to do whatever it took to survive.

He had his finger curled around the trigger when the two silhouetted figures appeared on the rim a little ways down the draw. The one called Buck had his rifle angled down. His pard, Rio, gripped a six-gun ready in his fist. They went taut as they saw only the empty floor of the gully under their guns.

"Right here, cowboys," Stark said softly. "But don't try it."

He was wasting his words, but he'd had to make the effort. Both of them swiveled toward him with the trained reflexes of experienced mankillers. Rio was closest, and his revolver only had to come around in a short arc to be in line. Stark's finger squeezed the trigger. The shotgun kicked like a mustang. At that range the spreading charge of buckshot caught them both. Through the eye-stinging cloud of smoke, Stark saw Rio go reeling against Buck, who plunged headfirst into the gully.

Instantly Stark came up into a crouch, the butt of the shotgun against his shoulder, the sights set square on the remaining member of the first pair he'd spotted. The other was down, caught by one of Buck's or Rio's bullets when they'd opened fire. The final hombre was on his knees beside the wounded man, face stricken with shock.

"Drop the iron or I'll cut you in half!" Stark rapped. "It's a solid load. Be like getting hit by a cannon."

The six-gun fell leadenly from the outlaw's fist.

Stark cast a sideward glance at the two fallen bushwhackers. Both of them were finished.

"How bad's your friend hit?" he demanded of his prisoner.

"Don't know," the fellow stammered. "But he's bleeding plenty."

Stark sighed as he straightened to his full height, lowering the shotgun a bit, but still keeping it on his captive. The hunt was over, he mused wearily. Now there were bodies to bury, and a long trek back to Guthrie with a prisoner and a wounded man in tow.

Chapter One

"You're a regular one-man posse, James," U.S. Marshal Evett Nix said as he ushered Stark to one of the straight-back chairs in front of his neatly kept desk. "Rio and Buck, the two you left out there, were trouble on the hoof. The Territory and the Lands are well rid of them. And you managed to bring back the other two culprits as well as the money. The bankers will be pleased."

"Came mighty close to working out different," Stark said, brushing the compliments aside, although the head lawman's praise meant a lot to him.

A former retail merchant, bank receiver, and grocer, Nix had been appointed marshal by the president of the United States more for his administrative abilities than for his prowess as a peace officer. Charged with bringing law and order to the Territory while keeping the politicos in Washington happy, Nix needed skills in both realms. Relying on the advice of some of the veteran lawmen

11

reporting to him, Nix had done a credible job of reining in the outlaw depredations taking place in his jurisdiction. Now, even the old-time lawdogs bore a genuine respect for him.

Nix straightened his tailored coat and ran a finger along his waxed handlebar mustache as he regarded Stark from across his desk. "You sure you won't consider giving up this private operative business of yours and signing on as one of my deputies?"

Stark grinned. "Pay me my standard retainer, and you can pin on the badge right now."

Nix shook his head ruefully. "Don't think Washington would approve my voucher for those kind of expenses."

Stark settled back in his chair and stretched his long legs out in front of him. He wore his customary city garb of corduroy coat, white shirt, string tie, and sharply creased pants. He had yet to replace the bullet-punctured Stetson. He placed it on the floor beside his chair.

Only his shotgun was absent from his usual armament. For all of being territorial capital and having the federal court and U.S. Marshal's Office located there, the city of Guthrie could still be a rowdy place, particularly for a man whose reputation made him a target for any yahoo looking to cut a sizable notch on the butt of his gun.

"Got your message over at my office, Stark drawled once he was comfortable. "Who's this fellow you want me to meet?"

A long soak in a hot tub at the hotel where he roomed and a good night's sleep had rid Stark of the grime and exhaustion of the trail. After a big breakfast in the hotel dining room, he had legged it to his office. The note he had found awaiting him there had brought him across the brick street to the Herriott Building where Nix had his office.

"Name's Andrew Blaine. He's on his way over now,

I expect,'' the marshal said in answer to Stark's query.
''He's been here in town a few days waiting for you, so
when the boys over at the jail reported you'd dropped
off a couple of new boarders last night, I took the liberty
of setting up a confab for this morning. Hope it didn't
get in the way of any plans.''

Stark shook his head. ''Nope. Just a routine report to
the Bankers Association. Reckon it can wait a spell.''
Silently he wondered just who this Blaine fellow was
that he had the U.S. Marshal arranging meetings for him.

''Here he is now,'' Nix announced before Stark could
give voice to the query.

The man who entered the office was short and broad,
with an air of aggressive strength that reminded Stark of
a purebred bull. He wore a finely cut suit, but looked as
though he'd be equally comfortable in cowpuncher's
gear. The lines of his full face bespoke a shrewd
strength. Aging, but still a man to ride the river with,
Stark judged.

He stood up and accepted a hard grip from Blaine's
compact hand as Nix made the introductions.

''James Stark,'' Blaine echoed as they were seated.
''Known as the Peacemaker because of that hogleg you
pack, and because you do business under that name.
Peacemaker: For Hire.''

''The marshal says you wanted to see me.''

''I think you may be of service to myself and the
fellows I represent,'' Blaine explained. ''We've done
some checking on you. You're a former Pinkerton operative, with all the scientific crime detection training
they give their best men. You have a reputation as a top
hand with most weapons, and as a good man for a friend,
but a bad man to cross. You've put in time as everything
from a lawman to a bounty hunter, and you hire out your
services as a troubleshooter, range detective, bodyguard,
and confidential investigator.''

"True enough, I reckon," Stark conceded. "But if you've checked on me, you know my services don't come cheap. And they don't necessarily go to the highest bidder."

Blaine was nodding before Stark finished. "We're aware of your fees, and we're ready to pay them. And we also know about your commitment to only take jobs that won't put you afoul of the law."

"It's more than that," Stark said coolly. "I won't work for any man or group of men who are involved in actions I can't abide, whether those actions are legal or not."

"That's one of the reasons we want to hire you. At times you've even worked for free when you were strongly opposed to what unscrupulous or ruthless men were doing. Such as the time up north when an Eastern consortium was trying to drive some independent coal miners out of business. Before the dust had settled, the consortium had pulled out, lock, stock and barrel, minus a couple of hired guns."

Stark glanced briefly at Evett Nix. Blaine and his cohorts had been doing some snooping, all right. "I've never gotten crossways of the law in any way that counted."

"And we're not asking you to do it now," Blaine asserted.

"Just who is it that's asking?" Stark decided it was time he needed to know.

"We're not a formal organization, not like the Mutual Protection Association or the Anti Horse-Thief Association. What we are is a loose group of ranchers leasing land from the tribes for pasture up in the northern region of Indian Territory."

Stark gave a nod of understanding. The practice wasn't uncommon. The tribes derived considerable income from it, although some less principled cattlemen had been known to take an Indian woman as wife just to have an unlimited claim to lands held by her tribe. He wondered if there were any such among Blaine's cronies. "I'm listening," he said.

"Reckon you know the problems men like us face. The larger our herds, the more likely we are to be hit by rustlers and such. And we have to depend mostly on ourselves for law enforcement."

Stark hiked his shoulders in a shrug. "That's nothing new. Big spreads like those in the Lands have always had to put up with a few wide-loopers."

"It's more than just a few wide-loopers," Blaine said, then amended his statement. "At least, we're fretting that it could be."

"Meaning what?"

"Ever heard of Dirk Garland, Mr. Stark?"

Stark frowned. "Runs a gang that used to cut a wide swath up Kansas way. Last I heard, he was trying to settle down now that things are getting respectable in those parts."

Blaine's face was bleak. "We've got word he and his outfit have moved into the Lands."

"What kind of word?"

"Just rumors mostly, up until the other day."

"What happened then?"

"One of my men—a good hand—used to work the ranches in Kansas. He knows Garland by sight. Well, he was up in the backcountry after some strays when he stumbled on a big camp. At least twenty men—a hard-looking crew, he said. And there was Garland, big as life, plumb in the middle of them."

"He's sure?" Stark demanded.

Blaine nodded. "No question about it."

"And they just let him ride out?"

"He said it was touch and go for a minute. Several of them were fingering their irons, and he figured he'd

ridden down the wrong trail for sure. Then Garland ordered them to let him alone. He skedaddled right fast.''

Stark cut an inquiring gaze at Nix.

"It checks out," the marshal confirmed. "When
Blaine here came to me with his story, I sent off a few
wires. Got the answers yesterday. Seems Garland and all
his old gang, who he'd hired on as hands, had settled
down sort of peaceable on a big spread he bought up
near Sedalia. The local authorities never had nothing
they could pin on him, so there wasn't much they could
do except stand by and keep an eye on him, even though
they were sure he'd bought that ranch with loot from
some of his raids.''

Sedalia, Kansas, Stark mused as dark memories
stirred. Tawdry queen of the old cattle towns. A fitting
place for the likes of Dirk Garland to hang up his guns.

But had he hung them up for good?

"And now he's on the prod again?" he questioned
aloud.

"Nobody knows," Nix responded. "Seems he and
most of his old gang up and rode out from his spread a
month or so back, leaving a few cowhands in charge.
Didn't even tell them where he was headed.''

"What set him off?"

Nix shrugged. "Anybody's guess. Some say it was
what happened to his son.''

"His son?" Stark echoed.

"A regular young hellion trying to follow in his pa's
footsteps," Nix elaborated. "His ma was a saloon floozy
who died of the consumption. He went to live with Garland, who wanted him to ride the straight and narrow.
The kid didn't take to it. He ain't much over sixteen,
and he's got a mind of his own. Started running with a
wild group, killed a man in a shooting scrap, then finally
got himself caught taking part in a bank robbery where

a couple of customers were shot down in cold blood. Word is, the kid pulled the trigger on one of them.''

''Where is he now?''

''In jail in Kansas with the rest of his sorry bunch awaiting trial.''

Stark chewed it over, conscious of Nix's shrewd eyes on him. None of it made much sense. Why would Garland hit the owlhoot trail again just because his son had gone bad?

He shifted his attention to Blaine. ''Any sign Garland is rustling your cattle?''

''There's no sign he's doing much of anything except staying holed up back in the hills. It's making folks in our parts mighty nervous.''

''Any trouble with him or his men?''

''Nope. He seems to be keeping them all on a real tight rein.''

''He's not breaking any laws,'' Nix added. ''Even if I did have any jurisdiction over the Lands, there ain't much I could do.''

Stark regarded Blaine levelly. ''Who else you got siding you?''

Blaine named a few names. Stark nodded a couple of times. He had heard of most of the men Blaine mentioned. A hardy breed, they had set up successful ranching operations in a lawless realm. The ones who negotiated with the tribes for a fair lease price were the upright ones. But in addition to the scoundrels preying off their Indian wives, there were those who simply moved in and claimed a sizable piece of the range, relying on their hired guns to keep it against the claims of whichever tribe actually owned the land.

Knowing that any direct aciton against such interlopers would only be characterized as an Indian uprising, with resultant harsh consequences, the Indians could only appeal for help to the very U.S. Cavalry that had conquered them and confined them to the Lands in the first place. Rarely was such help forthcoming. The trespassers were left with pretty much of a free hand. Could that be Garland's game?

"You want me to learn what Garland's up to?" Stark asked out loud.

"That's about the size of it," Blaine admitted. "We don't want any trouble with him if it can be avoided, but we don't care to be caught with our gunbelts off if he starts stirring things up."

Stark cut another look at Nix. "Any objections?" It was only a formality, since he'd be operating in the Lands anyway, but Stark had long made it his policy to work with the law whenever he could.

"No objections." Nix's smile was tight. "Truth is, I'd like to know what he's up to myself. We've got enough to say grace over with outfits like the Daltons and Bill Doolin, without having to worry ourselves about Dirk Garland maybe deciding he wants to cross over into Oklahoma Territory."

Stark turned his gaze back to Blaine. "I'll be asking for a retainer up front before I go riding into the lion's den. I'll do my best to learn what brought Garland into these parts. That's the only promise I'll make."

Blaine nodded agreeably. "I'm prepared to pay you."

"I'll need a couple of days here in Guthrie to take care of a few things before I ride out again," Stark went on. "And I'd like to know more about the business arrangements of you and your associates."

"Why don't we have dinner tonight at my hotel, and I'll tell you all you want to know."

"Suits me."

"And if you need anybody to side you, we've got some good men riding for us. Not gunmen, but top hands just the same."

"Most generally I work alone," Stark said quietly. "But I'll keep it in mind."

"I'm sure you fellows can sort out the details tonight, then," Nix spoke up brusquely. "Now, Mr. Blaine, if you'll excuse us, I have some other matters to talk over with Mr. Stark."

Blaine didn't protest. Stark stood to grip his hand and settle on a time for dinner before Nix ushered the rancher out.

"Thanks for the referral," Stark said dryly as Nix resumed his seat behind the desk.

"I'll be wanting to know what all you find out," Nix advised, dropping a little bit of the bluff friendliness he had shown with Blaine. "Dirk Garland's bad medicine. I don't take to the notion of him snorting and stomping in my bailiwick."

Stark nodded. He hadn't expected much else. Evett Nix wasn't in the habit of acting as his business broker just out of the goodness of his heart. In addition to having the potentially influential Blaine owing him a favor, Nix would expect a full report from Stark of his findings.

A tentative knock at the door made Nix frown. "What is it?" he called.

A clerkish type slipped into the office, handed Nix a sheet of paper, glanced at Stark with curious eyes, then retreated. Nix's frown deepened into a scowl as he read. He looked up at Stark.

"You've got trouble snapping at your heels, amigo."

"What kind of trouble?"

"I may have to lock you up for dropping the hammer on those two hombres riding with Rio and Buck."

Stark sat up straight in his chair. "Not funny, pard," he advised levelly.

Nix rattled the paper. "It's no joke."

"What the deuce are you talking about?"

"You know Damon Rasters?"

"Yeah. He's the new federal prosecutor sent here from back East when the Organic Act established a federal court for Oklahoma Territory."

Nix nodded solemnly. "Word is, he's going to have a warrant issued for your arrest this afternoon. Rio and Buck are claiming you bushwhacked them and backshot their two cohorts."

"And he's listening to them?" Stark exclaimed in disbelief.

Nix shrugged. "He's out to make a name for himself, and he doesn't like bounty hunters and vigilantes. That's pretty much what he considers you to be."

"But even if that hogwash about backshooting was true," Stark protested, "It all happened in the Indian Lands."

"Rasters claims he's got jurisdiction there by virtue of the Organic Act."

"That's loco!"

Nix shrugged again. "Who knows, these days? Rasters has filed suit with the U.S. Supreme Court seeking to have the Act interpreted his way. Until there's a ruling, he's acting like they've already decided in his favor. And there's no one to gainsay him. I didn't think he'd go this far, though."

"What's his game?"

"Like I told you, he's got his eye on higher offices than federal prosecutor of this territory. If the court decides for him, he will have made a big name for himself. In the meantime, you're well enough known hereabouts that it would put a mighty nice feather in his cap to rope and hogtie you."

Stark chewed it over. It tasted bitter. The idea of spending time in a cell, even temporarily, didn't set well with him. And it wouldn't do his business any good either.

"I can put in a good word for you," Nix advised,

"But I doubt Rasters will pay much attention. He hasn't in the past. I suggest you get yourself a lawyer, pronto."

Stark lifted hard eyes to him. "You got anybody to recommend?"

"Most lawyers around here would as soon steer clear of Rasters, just in case he ends up as governor or some such. There's only two of them who've had much luck bucking him."

"Who are they?"

"One of them's Temple Houston."

Stark knew of the flamboyant son of Sam Houston, whose reputation for courtroom dramatics was matched by his proven prowess with a six-gun. "Blowhard," he said dismissively.

"You won't like the other one any better," Nix predicted.

"What's his name?"

"*Her* name," Nix corrected dryly. "Prudence Mc-Kay."

"A woman!" Stark burst out.

"Yep, but don't sell her short. She's good at what she does."

"When did she blow into town?" Stark asked sourly.

"A few months back. Surprised you haven't run into her before now."

"I'd just as soon forgo the pleasure. Somehow, I can't see no woman shyster getting me out of this."

"Give her a chance," Nix suggested. "You might be surprised in more ways than one. I've seen her work. She's not short on spunk, and she's got plenty of savvy to go along with it."

"How did she ever become a lawyer?"

"Runs in the family, I guess. Her dad's a judge up in Kansas. I did some checking on her background when she showed up here. She attended Cornell University, went to Cincinnati Law School, then got her law degree from the University of Michigan. Don't know if her pa pulled any strings on her behalf or not. I tend to doubt it howsomever. None of the other shysters around here have dared to question her credentials. She's better qualified than most of them, and they know it.''

Stark shook his head in wonderment. He had heard of lady lawyers back East, but had never come across one in the Territory. Most men who pursued a legal career in these parts had studied in the East, or worked under the tutelage of established territorial lawyers, before passing a sorry bar exam, rife with cronyism, which consisted largely of informal questioning by a select panel of established local practitioners.

The heady pioneer atmosphere of Oklahoma, coupled with the wide-open lifestyle most folks had, bred plenty of disputes over everything from boundary lines to gambling to horse stealing. When blazing pistols didn't settle the issue, the lawyers found fertile ground to ply their trade.

But apparently none of them were any too eager to lock horns with Damon Rasters.

"How much time do I have?'' Stark heard himself ask resignedly.

"I can drag my feet a little bit, but once the warrant's issued, I'll have to put out an order to bring you in.'' Nix sighed with genuine regret. "Sorry, James. Nothing else I can do.''

"Yeah,'' Stark said bleakly. He wondered just what, if anything, he himself could do.

Chapter Two

The letters stenciled on the frosted glass door read, PRUDENCE MCKAY, ATTORNEY AND COUNSELOR AT LAW. Stark hesitated before reaching for the knob. The notion of going to a female lawyer for help still rankled. But the bit of checking he'd been able to do had confirmed Nix's assessment. The new federal prosecutor had most other lawyers hereabouts buffaloed. Miss Prudence McKay looked to be his best bet.

The brick street outside had been busy with the usual clutter of pedestrians, riders, horsedrawn vehicles, and the occasional horseless carriage. One of Nix's deputies—a man known vaguely to Stark—ambled past with a brief nod of acknowledgment. If Nix's info was right, then before too much longer, that fellow and all his star-packing compatriots would have orders to arrest him on sight, Stark mused grimly.

He reached for the knob.

A bell rang as he entered. He found himself in a small

waiting area that was simply but tastefully furnished. A vase of fresh wildflowers was a distinctively feminine touch. An open doorway led to a connecting office.

There was a rustle of movement, and then a lovely young woman in a high-necked dress of dark fabric appeared in the doorway. Stark caught his breath. He had an impression of a full figure that not even the severe attire could conceal, of brunette hair pulled conservatively up on top of her head, and dark brown eyes that rested on him steadily.

"Yes? May I help you?" Her voice was courteous and pleasant, but nothing more.

Stark didn't know what he'd expected in Prudence McKay, but this sure wasn't it. "My name's James Stark." He found his voice, doffing his Stetson belatedly. "I may need a lawyer. Evett Nix suggested I see you."

Something had flickered in her brown eyes at the mention of his name, but she inclined her head in a civil fashion and gestured him forward. "Very well. Won't you come into my office?" As she turned to precede him, he fancied that a faint flush had touched her comely features for some reason.

Her face was a composed mask, however, by the time she was seated facing him across her desk. Like the foyer, her office was tastefully furnished, with a woman's touch here and there. A massive rolltop desk against one wall looked to be her work station. Several neat stacks of folders were arranged on it.

"Tell me why you think you need a lawyer, Mr. Stark."

She was all business, and it dawned on Stark for the first time just how hard it must've been for a woman, a young attractive one in particular, to make it through the Eastern law schools and then establish a practice in this rowdy territory. Nix had described her as having plenty of spunk and savvy. That might not cover the half of it, Stark realized.

"Well, Mr. Stark?"

"I do some work for the Bankers Association," Stark began awkwardly.

"I'm aware of your . . . shall we say . . . line of work, Mr. Stark," she said, cutting him off with a trace of disapproval. "Just tell me why you're here."

"I have it on pretty solid authority that the prosecutor's going to issue a warrant for my arrest before the day's out."

Her composure didn't slip. "Go on."

As briefly as he could, Stark related the events of the manhunt in the Indian Lands. He caught her gaze as he finished, but her eyes flicked quickly away from his.

The firm set of her full lips seemed to soften momentarily, but her tone was brisk. "Describe the gunfight."

Stark felt suddenly uncomfortable talking of killing to this fetching woman. "I got the drop on two of them but the other pair was waiting for me. They threw down on me, and I had to return fire."

She frowned. "No, Mr. Stark. Tell me in detail exactly what happened."

Stark reined in his jumbled emotions and complied with her request. He described the gunbattle as if he was testifying in court, which he'd done more than once. She listened attentively, jotting notes on a pad, asking occasional questions that would've done a prosecutor proud.

"You were in the gully, and they were turning toward you when you fired at them from an upward angle with your shotgun?" she asked probingly once he was done.

Stark shifted in his hard chair. "That's right."

"Is that the hat you were wearing?"

"Yes, ma'am."

"Let me see it."

He came half out of his chair to extend it to her. She appeared a bit flustered as she reached to retrieve it, bringing her closer to him across the desktop. She settled back in her chair and examined the battered headwear closely, even lifting it up to squint through the aligned bullet holes.

At last she set it on her desk and faced him squarely. "As I said, Mr. Stark, I know of your trade, and I do not approve of it. Such work smacks of vigilantism, of taking the law into your hands, and of hiring your gun out to the highest bidder. A society that allows such activities cannot survive. However, you are entitled to legal representation, and I will do my best to provide it. In this instance, I believe Mr. Rasters has overstepped his authority, and that you are being unjustly charged."

She paused to glance at a fine Gilbert clock on her desk. "I want you to meet me at the prosecutor's office in two hours." She eyed him gaugingly. "Come dressed as you are, but do not wear your pistol or that knife. We want to make the proper impression. And . . . bring your hat. Is that clear?"

"Yes, ma'am," Stark said like a schoolboy to the teacher.

"Then I will see you shortly. Good day."

Fighting a scowl, Stark took his leave. *The high-handed, overeducated little filly!* he fumed. But he'd put himself in her hands now. He only hoped she was as good as Evett Nix said.

The whole business still rankled two hours later when he met her in the hallway of the Herriott Building, which housed the U.S. Prosecutor's den along with other official offices.

He had shucked his Peacemaker and bowie, but the Marlin .38 still rode snugly at his back. He'd switched the holster to the waistline of his whipcord pants.

Prudence McKay eyed him up and down, then nodded

her approval. Stark eyed her back, and she flushed and dropped her eyes. He saw, with a little bit of surprise, that she wasn't a tall woman—she was almost small, as a matter of fact. The force of her willful personality gave her a presence that belied her stature.

That same personality, and what Stark took to be grudging respect, got them past a pack of clerical and bookkeeper sorts, to be ushered into the spacious and lavishly furnished chambers of Damon Rasters.

The federal prosecutor was a slender waspish man, still young, whose bearing and attire were better suited for some boardroom or courthouse back East. He was a dude, right enough, but in his sharp nervous movements and the almost feverish glitter of his eyes, Stark read a ruthless ambition.

"I'm a busy man, Miss McKay. It's an imposition to spare you even a few minutes of my time."

"This shouldn't take long, Mr. Prosecutor, and might save you time in the long run. I understand you intend to bring charges against my client, Mr. James Stark."

Rasters looked at Stark, acknowledging him for the first time, and sniffed disdainfully. "You are uncommonly well informed, Miss McKay." He remained standing, facing them across his desk. Prudence McKay stayed on her feet as well. Stark had the impression he was watching two prizefighters square off in a ring where there weren't too awful many rules.

"Exactly what charges are you planning to have pressed against Mr. Stark?"

"Murder," Rasters said flatly with a sharp glance at Stark.

"Whose murder?" she demanded.

"A man known as Rio Sanders, and his companion, Buck Epworth."

"What evidence do you have?"

"The testimony of two eyewitnesses."

"And just who are your witnesses?"

"Jake Newstrom and Nate Plunker."

"Who goes by Kid Lefty, if I'm not mistaken."

Rasters bridled, then squared his slender shoulders. "That's correct."

Her eyes flashed. "He's wanted for cattle rustling; Jake Newstrom's cut from the same cheap cloth. Both of them are in jail. I've spoken with them at some length." She shook her head in evident disgust. "You've got yourself a fine pair of witnesses, Mr. Rasters. How do you think they'd look to a jury, particularly after I cross-examine them?"

"They are innocent until proven guilty, Miss McKay. Or have you forgotten that fine point of law? Further, their sworn testimony is entitled to due weight in a court of law, and is sufficient evidence for charges to be brought against that man!" He stabbed an accusatory finger in Stark's direction, but didn't seem too eager to look directly at him again.

"Exactly what was the content of their sworn testimony?" McKay pressed.

If possible, Rasters stood even more stiffly. "They stated they were camped with the two decedents when your client appeared and opened fire without warning, shooting Mr. Sanders and Mr. Epworth in the back, and wounding Mr. Plunker. Mr. Newstrom pleaded for both their lives, and your client relented from murdering them as well."

Stark bit back the cutting interruption that rose to his lips. His attorney seemed to be doing fine without his help.

"Mr. Stark was hired by the Bankers Association to bring in four bank robbers," she said evenly. "The Association will confirm that for you. They set a great deal of store by him. He tracked your witnesses and their accomplices from the bank into the Indian Lands. Kid

Lefty and Newstrom were set to bushwhack him. He suspected it, so he circled and came up on them. When he told them to surrender, Epworth and Sanders opened fire on him from behind. One of them cocking a gun gave him an instant's warning. It was by God's grace that he was able to get them both, instead.''

Rasters sneered at her mention of the Deity. ''That is your client's version,'' he announced tightly, ''the self-serving version, I might add, of a man known to be little more than a gunslinger himself.''

''But just as entitled to due weight in a court of law as the self-serving statements of your witnesses,'' she reminded, and went on before he could react. ''You are aware, of course, that they had the bank money in their possession when he apprehended them.''

''They claim they found it.''

''And you believe them?''

''I have no good reason to doubt their story.''

Without looking at him, Mckay extended her hand to Stark. ''Your hat, please, Mr. Stark.'' With it in hand, she went on firmly. ''When their accomplices opened fire, they almost killed my client.'' Deftly she flicked the hat across the desk separating her from her opponent. To his credit, Rasters caught it. ''Check the bullet holes, Mr. Prosecutor. If you know anything about firearms, you'll see that the bullet that made them entered from the back of the crown, and exited from the front at a slightly different angle. That's because Mr. Stark was throwing himself to the ground at the time.''

''I know about firearms, Miss McKay,'' Rasters advised coldly, but he studied the punctured Stetson closely. Stark imagined a banker's calculating machine in his brain totaling up the odds of winning this case.

At last the prosecutor lifted his head and placed the hat carefully on his desk. ''This bullet hole could've been made at any time; your client could've made it himself to corroborate his story.''

''But it is evidence that's entitled to due weight in a court of law,'' McKay threw his own words back at him again. ''Do you still believe your witnesses?''

''It's my job to prosecute those suspected of crimes, Miss McKay.''

''There's a valid question as to whether you even have jurisdiction over this matter, assuming a crime was committed at all,'' she snapped. ''And your evidence is hardly conclusive. I suggest that we go back, exhume those bodies, and have a physician examine them to see if the bullet wounds were made from behind. Mr. Stark used buckshot—it shouldn't be too difficult to tell. The press would, no doubt, wish to send along a representative to cover this whole affair, once word of it leaked out. And the trial would attract national publicity, I'm sure.''

Paleness had crept over Raster's features. ''I hardly think that will be necessary.'' His nostrils flared. ''Perhaps my office will be willing to reconsider the charges. A junior prosecutor drew them up without consulting me, you understand.''

''Are you saying the charges will be dropped?''

''Under the circumstances, no warrant will be issued,'' Rasters said decisively, as if it was his own idea.

McKay nodded her pretty head with satisfaction. ''Then, we'll take no more of your time.''

Raster's face was unreadable as he watched them go.

''Congratulations, counselor,'' Stark said once he had followed her into the hall.

She wheeled on him. Fire flashed in her eyes. ''I do agree with Mr. Rasters on one thing,'' she stated. ''I still consider your trade as little more than that of a high-priced hired gun.''

Stark inclined his head. "I'm sorry you feel that way," he said honestly.

She appeared slightly taken aback. "Let me know if you have any further trouble with the prosecutor's office over this affair," she spoke quickly as if to cover whatever emotions had touched her.

"I'll do that," Stark promised. "And I appreciate your help."

"You'll get my bill," she said over her shoulder as she turned away.

Stark didn't doubt it. He watched her go, shaking his head in wonder. He remembered her flashing eyes, and found himself imagining how those same eyes would look if she saw a man as a beau and not a hired killer.

Surprised at himself, he shook the thought off. The last thing he needed was to go getting tangled up with a wildcat like Prudence McKay.

He was still musing over their meeting as he left the Herriott Building and headed toward his office, threading his way through the traffic. He mounted the stairs to the second floor, then pulled up abruptly as he saw the gun-slung shape leaning indolently against the wall beside his door in the dim corridor. Reflexively his hand moved toward the butt of the concealed .38.

"No need for that." The figure straightened lazily to face him. "Leastways, not yet."

Stark stepped closer to get a better look. "What's that supposed to mean?"

He couldn't recollect ever seeing the fellow before. Tall and stringy, with a bony face and mean little eyes that belied his easygoing stance, he kept his hand well clear of the iron holstered at his side. His clothes were nothing fancy, except for a fine pair of tooled boots that would've set a cowhand back several months' wages.

But this was no cowhand.

"You're the one they call the Peacemaker, ain't you?" he drawled.

"Do I know you?" Stark said without a trace of inflection.

The stranger inclined his head. "Not yet, you don't, but we got us some business to transact, you and me."

"That being?"

"I hear tell you buried a pard of mine the other day. Rio Sanders. That name ring a bell?"

Stark sighed. Putting that sorry hombre in the ground looked to be something that was going to haunt him for a spell, one way of the other, he concluded darkly.

"Sanders had it coming," he said aloud. "You got a problem with it?"

"Yeah. Yeah, I reckon I do. Folks know me as Brazos. I come here looking for my old pard, Rio, and then some ranny over't the saloon tells me you left him out in the Lands. That gives me a mighty big score to settle with you."

Word had traveled fast, Stark thought. And here was another two-bit gunslick looking to carve a notch in his reputation. A sudden reckless urge to have the matter out here and now rose in him, tautening his muscles and lifting the hairs on his nape.

Unexpectedly the pretty face of Prudence McKay flashed in his mind's eye, and he heard again the distaste in her tones. What had she named him? A hired gun. A worm twisted down in his gut. He'd had his bellyfull of killing for the nonce, he decided.

"So, folks know you as Brazos," he said, and heard the tightness in his voice. "Well, I don't know you as nothing, and I got no hankering to kill you. So just back off, and let it ride. Otherwise, the only score you'll be settling will likely be one with Old Nick himself. You savvy?"

"Don't much matter what your wants are, Peacemaker. There's a time and a place for us. I just want you to know that; just want you to sweat a little bit thinking about it. But that time ain't now, and the place ain't here. No, I want it to be public, so lots of folks can see the great Peacemaker go down under the gun of a better man.''

''The time and place won't make any difference,'' Stark said coldly. ''I've warned you once. Now, for the last time, ride clear of me, or you'll regret it.''

''We'll see who does the regretting. Be looking for me, Peacemaker. You'll see me coming. My word on it.''

Carefully Brazos backed away, holding his gunman's stance. When he reached the rear stairway, he lifted his left hand in a last mocking salute, then disappeared. Stark heard the clatter of his fancy boots on the stairs.

He sighed heavily, his shoulders sagging a bit. He had a nasty hunch Brazos was going to be a man of his word.

Chapter Three

Almost regretfully Prudence McKay closed the last folder and added it to the neat stack of files on her rolltop desk. She took a moment to lean back in her swivel chair. She was finished for the day, and in a sense she was sorry for that fact, because it left her at loose ends for the evening.

Sighing, she rose and slid the curved top down over the desk's surface. She turned about then and surveyed her office, wondering at the odd discontent which had settled gradually over her. After a rocky start, her law practice was going well, and she had turned a nice bit of business that very afternoon, which would be well reflected in the billing she sent to Mr. James Stark.

But still, the notion of another long evening occupied with law books and poetry in the hotel room where she lived left her spirit heavy.

Reluctantly she was forced to admit to herself that her disquiet might have its origins in the undeniable spark of attraction she had felt when her gaze first met that of James Stark, and the matching spark she was sure she had seen in his steely gray eyes.

Resolutely she put the disturbing perception aside and moved to do the last-minute straightening up of the office she always performed before closing for the day. But the unease still hovered on the fringes of her mind.

She had grown up occupied with meeting her father's stringent demands for achievement, as well as those even stricter ones she had imposed on herself; there had been little time for frivolous social activities or romantic entanglements with the eligible beaus who had pursued her. Of needs, her entire focus had been fixed on succeeding in the male realm of law school and then establishing her legal practice.

After disputes with her father over whether she should serve as his law clerk or open her own law office, she had moved rebelliously to Guthrie, partly to escape his dominion, and partly to prove that she did not need him, or his patronage as judge, to succeed in her career.

Well, succeed she had, she reminded herself, even to the extent of being able to outmaneuver U.S. Prosecutor Damon Rasters on his own turf. But the prideful thought did little to alleviate her sadness this evening.

James Stark was not a man to whom she could be seriously attracted, she asserted to herself as though putting forth a legal argument in the courtroom. He was arrogant and violent, almost as much of an outlaw as the disreputable men he hunted. The very idea of seeing him on any sort of a social, let alone, romantic, basis was absurd. To do so would be a betrayal of her own lofty principles, as well as the legal system to which she had devoted her life.

Finished with neatening up, she smoothed down her dress, checked her appearance automatically in the looking glass, extinguished the lamp, then let herself out into the hallway.

"Ah, Miss McKay. What a pleasant stroke of fortune to encounter you here."

She knew the voice. It was with mixed emotions that she turned toward the tall, lean-hipped figure striding confidently down the hall toward her. "Mr. Houston," she said in greeting.

"I've told you, it's Temple, please. We really should be on a first-name basis as fellow members of the bar."

He halted, towering over her, his fetching smile flashing above his chiseled jaw. A long mane of auburn hair flowed to his shoulders.

Son of General Sam Houston, first and only president of the Republic of Texas, Temple Houston had a reputation as a gunfighter, a skilled lawyer, and something of a gentleman rake. All these aspects of his character were reflected in his customary garb of Prince Albert coat, costly Spanish-style vest, and satin-striped trousers flaring over Texas riding boots. A pearl-handled revolver was holstered at his waist. He had doffed his white Stetson as he addressed her.

His courtroom antics were legendary. Once, in order to demonstrate the speed of which a skilled gunman was capable, he had suddenly pulled a pair of six-guns, loaded with blanks, and emptied them at the unsuspecting jury. This effort at proving that his client had acted reasonably in shooting first when confronted by a gunman was unsuccessful, however, and his client was convicted. Undaunted, Houston had won an appeal for a new trial on the grounds that the jurors, while scattering to avoid his blazing guns, had mingled with onlookers and bystanders, and thus had not been sequestered as required by law.

"I was just leaving, sir," Prudence told him now with formal politeness.

"As was I, when I spied you." His talent for flowery oratory showed even in casual conversation. "It occurred to me that you might consider joining me in the evening's repast." He flashed his charming smile again.

To her surprise, Prudence found herself hesitating. She had managed to fend off previous invitations from him, but, just now, the prospect of dinner in his thoroughly masculine company held a tempting allure.

"We'll dine at your hotel," Houston pressed, as if sensing her wavering resolve. "It won't be out of your way at all, and you will have greatly brightened my evening by your company."

"Very well," Prudence heard herself say, and wondered what in the world had gotten into her.

His gray eyes lit up. Courteously he offered his arm, and, with no recourse, she laid a hand demurely on his coat sleeve and allowed herself to be escorted from the building.

He *was* charming, she was forced to admit as they made their way the short distance to her hotel. He kept up an entertaining discourse on topics ranging from the local political situation to current plays and authors back East, and his humorous views of mutual acquaintances. More than once she caught herself smiling at some particularly clever witticism. Almost unconsciously she let her hand rest a little more firmly on his arm, until she could feel the solidity of his muscles beneath the fabric of his coat.

In the restaurant—one of Guthrie's finest—he was just as gallant in seating her and ordering for them both after a brief consultation with her. When the maître d' suggested wine, Houston paused, glanced at her, then declined. He was certainly adept in discerning her wishes, she mused.

Watching him, she found herself wondering how the manners of James Stark would compare with her present companion's polished etiquette. Probably not well at all, she concluded. Stark was an uncouth gunfighter, and would, no doubt, be completely out of place in these elegant surroundings.

"This is an odd occasion for daydreaming," Houston's teasing voice intruded on her reverie.

"Oh, I'm sorry," she apologized quickly, hoping she wouldn't blush. "I was just doing a little woolgathering." Why in heaven's name had she been thinking about James Stark? she asked herself angrily.

"I understand you put our esteemed federal prosecutor in his place this afternoon."

So the story was already out, she thought with a touch of professional pride. "Mr. Roster set himself up for it by proposing to bring some unfounded charges against my client," she replied modestly.

"James Stark was your client. Correct?"

"Why, yes. What do you think of him?" Immediately she could've pinched herself for asking the question.

"Stark?" Houston said with some surprise. "A high-dollar hired gun." He spoke dismissively. "He's reputed to operate under some rigid moral code of his own, but I tend to doubt it."

Prudence took a welcome sip of her tea. "Oh? Why is that?" she said in tones she hoped conveyed only passing interest.

Houston shrugged. "Most men of his ilk have moral codes which are very flexible when it comes to seeing the viewpoint of the highest bidder for their services."

"And on what do you base your opinion?" She tried to keep her tones light, but guessed from the narrowing of his eyes that she hadn't quite succeeded.

"On experience," he answered. "I've dealt with men like him. Basically, they are barbarians, whose first and only solution to a problem is gunplay." He brushed back his coat to reveal the pearl handle of his holstered pistol.

He rested his palm on it. "Sometimes I've been forced to use a gun to settle matters, but a truly civilized man is one who will only use a gun as a last resort."

"And have you ever met Mr. Stark?"

"We don't move in the same circles, I'm afraid." Houston frowned abruptly. "Now, what's this? Here I invite a lovely young woman to dinner, and she only wishes to spend the evening discussing another man."

Prudence had the grace to drop her eyes as she sensed the flush rising to her face. "How inconsiderate of me," she murmured contritely, then raised her eyes. "Please do forgive me."

His white teeth gleamed in his smile. "But, of course, dear lady. You need not even ask. All is forgiven." Then he looked past her and his lips twisted sardonically. "Why, speak of old Lucifer himself," he growled.

Prudence twisted about in her chair to see the tall, unmistakable figure of James Stark wending his way past the other occupied tables. He was in the company of the maître d' and a short, solidly built man who had the stamp of a rancher. Stark seemed to be selecting their table himself. His eyes swept over the restaurant. Prudence thought she saw them widen at the sight of her, then narrow as they fell on her companion. Hastily she put her attention back on Houston. To her frustration, he was regarding her shrewdly.

"So, the Peacemaker seems to have made quite an impression," he commented.

"Nonsense. He's a new client. Nothing more."

Wisely, Houston held his tongue, and Prudence busied herself with her meal. Between ladylike morsels of her steak, she tried to turn the conversation to various legal matters of common concern. Houston listened and commented appropriately.

Prudence did her best to keep her attention on him, but she was all too aware that the waiter had seated Stark and the rancher at a nearby table that she could observe out of the corner of her eye with only a slight movement of her head.

She couldn't help but notice that Stark seemed quite at home in the environment of the fine restaurant. He didn't eat with his fingers, put his boots on the table, or pick his teeth with his bowie knife. She wondered about the subject of the earnest conversation he was having with the rancher. Their voices were inaudible to her. She questioned whether Stark was surreptitiously observing her, then told herself it was unimportant.

Dessert was some of the exotic ice cream that was still new to the Territory, and available only in the nicer establishments here in the capital. Prudence spooned hers daintily to her lips, unable to stop the delightful shiver that raced over her at each taste of the delicious confection.

Houston had grown quiet, and she fancied she caught his eyes cast in Stark's direction on more than one occasion. She had just excavated another spoonful of the ice cream when she saw Houston go rigid.

At the same moment, a man's voice rang harshly across the restaurant. ''Peacemaker!

As she turned her head toward the sound, she spotted a tall bony stranger, clad in range gear, threading his way smoothly past the tables toward Stark. A holstered pistol was at his side, and one hand hovered menacingly over it.

''Peacemaker!'' You and I got a score to settle! You gunned down my pard! I told you there'd be a time and a place for us. Well, this is it. Here and now, in front of all these fine folks, so they can see the Peacemaker go down to a better man!''

Stark was on his feet. He had been seated facing the entrance—by design, Prudence realized now—and he stepped away from the table to await the newcomer, motioning the rancher to stay clear.

Prudence had half-risen from her chair when she felt a firm hand close on her shoulder and draw her down behind the shelter of the table. "Keep low!" Houston's tense voice ordered. "This could get ugly."

It already was ugly. All about, other patrons were ducking and scrambling for cover. The stranger pushed a table unceremoniously aside to clear a space between him and Stark. Irrelevantly, Prudence saw that he wore expensive hand-tooled boots.

"People! Listen up! My name is Brazos!" the stranger shouted in a shrill voice. "You remember that name. Remember what you're fixing to see here tonight. A legend's going to die. A new one's being born. What about it, Peacemaker? You ready to settle up?"

"I already told you." Stark's cool tones carried clearly. "I got no call to fight you."

"I say different!" Brazos was still shouting. "But if you need a reason, I'll give you one. You fight me, or I'll kill you where you stand." He gave a harsh bark of laughter. "Shoot, I'll kill you no matter what you do!"

Stark's eyes flickered briefly about the room. Prudence could've sworn they touched on her where she crouched with Temple Houston.

"Lots of folks in here," Stark observed reasonably. "You want to fight, let's take it outside. Otherwise, some of these people might get hurt."

"No! We do it in here, where everybody can see!"

Stark's face hardened. The planes and angles of it stood out clearly. Prudence felt a chill as if she'd just taken another bite of the ice cream melting in its bowl on the table.

"Okay." Subtly, oddly, Stark shifted his feet so that his left side was turned just a bit toward his opponent.

His hands, half-closed, hovered at waist level. "You're asking for a fight; I reckon you got it."

"What are you doing?" Brazos cried. "Why are you standing like that? Get ready to pull your iron!"

"You fixing to draw," came Stark's mocking tones, "Or are you just going to stand there and run off at the mouth?"

Brazos spat an oath. With the foul word, his hand stabbed down toward his holstered gun and pulled it clear of leather. As it came up, Stark slid forward so rapidly that Prudence's eye could hardly register the movement. He made no effort to pull his own gun. His fisted hands lifted almost like those of a prizefighter, and his left leg, held straight as a fence post, swept across so that the edge of his boot caught Brazos's gun as it came level. The impact tore the weapon from his fingers and sent it sailing across the wide room.

Stark's foot didn't touch down. His extended leg flexed at the knee, then snapped back in the opposite direction, driving his boot against Brazos's shoulder so his gun arm dropped limp at his side. As his foot met the floor at last, Stark's fists flashed in a series of punches as fast as the double kick that had preceded them. Brazos spun halfway about before his knees buckled and he collapsed awkwardly. The heel of one expensive boot briefly drummed the floor, then was still.

"Savate!" Houston hissed sharply at Prudence's side.

"What?"

"*Boxe Française savate.*" The French rolled fluently from Houston's tongue. He was staring intently at Stark as he spoke. "The Frenchmen combined their own style of foot fighting with English pugilism. In London, I saw a savate fighter defeat an English boxer. Our Mr. Stark is apparently an expert."

"And a civilized man," Prudence whispered, almost to herself. He used his gun only as a last resort.

Houston might not have heard her. Still observing Stark, he straightened to his feet and holstered his revolver. Prudence hadn't seen him draw it. She rose alongside him as Stark shifted his attention their way.

"Thanks for the thought." Stark nodded at Houston's waist, and Prudence understood that, somehow, he must've noted the lawyer's drawn gun even during the heat of action.

"Just protecting the lady," Houston answered easily.

Stark nodded. "Sorry to interrupt your dinner, Miss McKay."

"I'm glad you weren't hurt, Mr. Stark," she replied in a voice that was thankfully steady.

"One of the hazards of being a hired gun," he responded dryly, then turned back to the fallen gunman. "I better make sure all his fangs are pulled." Kneeling, he began a quick search of his victim.

Prudence glimpsed a man wearing a deputy's badge headed toward the disturbance through the press of onlookers. Then Temple Houston's commanding grip turned her away from the scene. "Perhaps an after-dinner might soothe your nerves," he suggested suavely.

"No, thank you," Prudence said. "I think I'll adjourn to my room. Court's in recess for the evening."

And, she reflected, the jury was still out on her opinion of James Stark.

Chapter Four

The disreputable community of Corner, located just across Hell's Fringe from Indian Territory, owed its existence to a single saloon. Around this establishment had grown up a sorry collection of ramshackle structures occupied by an even sorrier bunch of citizens ranging from cattle rustlers to hired killers, soiled doves, and bootleg whiskey peddlers.

At dusk, Stark rode past the small weed-infested cemetery without stopping. He had seen it before. He had even been responsible for planting one of its residents there a spell back.

A few of the graves bore sad, tilting crosses. Most of them were unmarked. They were filled largely by nameless victims of murders and gunfights at the saloon. The South Canadian River, winding close past the graveyard and the town, was said to sometimes run red with blood when the saloon got rowdy. One day, Stark mused, the dark waters of the river might carry away the cemetery and even the town itself, leaving only a few bones for passersby to wonder at a century from now. Good riddance, he figured.

But trouble towns like Corner, and the nearby Violet Springs, had their uses. In particular, Stark had found Corner to be a good site for picking up a cold trail. Lawless scavengers from both sides of the border congregated there to lie low, carouse, or pick up supplies, oftentimes on the run. For a man who knew how to get it, information was available, as well.

Stark was an old hand at getting information. He reined up at the saloon. A pair of hard cases loitered in front of it. Stark met their gauging stares with one of his own, and they were the first to look away. Stark kept a wary eye on them as he dismounted. Down an alley, he glimpsed a bar girl stooping over the sprawled form of a snoring, drunken cowhand. The yahoo would wake up with a hangover and not a cent to his name, Stark reflected grimly. He'd be lucky to be alive. Run-of-the-mill goings-on for Corner.

The two hard cases gave way as he entered the saloon. One of them bore a look of dawning recognition. It was tinged with fright.

Stark had left the unrepentant Brazos locked up in one of Evett Nix's jail cells. After reviewing some of the marshal's old records, he'd loaded Red in a boxcar and taken a train west for Hell's Fringe. Disembarking at nearby Asher, he headed the sorrel stallion toward Corner.

The ride had been peaceful, although hard experience made him keep his eyes peeled and watch his backtrail for trouble. He had taken such precautions for so long that he no longer thought much about them now. They were part of the price of his trade.

The fetching vision of Prudence McKay, as he'd last seen her at the hotel restaurant in Guthrie, persisted in keeping him company as he rode. He recalled the near-stricken look on her face as he'd turned away from the downed gunslinger, and he felt a moody regret that she had seen the incident. What must she think of him now, brawling in public places? Her opinion that he was a man of violence would only be heightened.

And how had he compared in her eyes to the dashing Temple Houston? he wondered sourly. Doubtless, he had come out a poor second best beside the gun-toting lawyer. Stark had never had much use for the son of the Texas president. And his feelings toward Houston hadn't improved any upon seeing him in the company of the comely Miss McKay. Stark had been surprised at the twinge of envy—and jealousy?—he'd felt on spotting the pair. But Houston had been ready enough to deal with trouble, Stark had to acknowledge. He'd give the shyster credit for that much, anyway.

And he needed to be ready to deal with trouble himself on this mission. He'd learned little more from Andrew Blaine at their dinner conference, although he'd made arrangements to meet with the ranch hand who claimed to have seen Dirk Garland's camp. That was set for tomorrow, over in the Lands. First, he wanted to see if any dust had been stirred up of late in the Corner Saloon.

He slid sideways out of the doorway as he entered so as not to frame himself there. Taking a moment, he surveyed the dim smoky interior. The familiar mingled smells of whiskey, sweat, and tobacco made his nostrils flare.

The cluttered room housed a motley collection of boozy cowpokes, cheap floozies, surly gunpackers, and a cardsharp or two. A few rickety gaming tables were being put to use. Stark felt eyes turn to him. There was more recognition in some, he knew, but, beyond a certain wariness on the part of the gunhands, nobody seemed to be on the prod. Just the same, he kept his hand near the Peacemaker as he threaded his way to the bar. The sodden sawdust on the floor clung damply to his boots.

A fallen woman with the body of a young girl and the ancient haunted eyes of a hag sidled up to him, but was waved peremptorily away by the bartender.

"What do you want here, Stark?" that worthy growled without warmth.

"A beer." Stark propped his left arm on the rough-hewn bar. "You're looking fine these days, Mort," he added sardonically.

The barkeep snorted derisively and turned away to fill his order. The proprietor of the Corner Saloon was a big hard man who carried a brace of mismatched revolvers stuck in the waistband of his apron, and a lead-filled sap in his back pocket. Stark knew he also kept a sawed-off shotgun under the bar. His bald head bore the scars of ancient brawls. It took a ruffian like Mort to run a dive like this.

Mort thudded a mug down in front of Stark. He sipped at it, then set it aside. He wasn't much of a drinker. Alcohol dulled the brain and the reflexes—a bad combination for a man who lived by the gun.

"Many strangers coming in lately?" he asked casually.

Mort shrugged. "They come and they go. Some I seen before. Some I ain't. What's it to you, anyway, Stark?"

"Heard there was some new blood on the other side of the Fringe. Thought they might be looking for a good hand."

"New blood? What the deuce are you talking about?"

Stark figured he may as well put his cards on the table. "Ever hear of Dirk Garland?" He watched Mort carefully as he spoke.

The barkeep frowned, making wrinkles rise far up on

his bald skull. "Kansas badman, ain't he? Never did run in these parts. Besides, I heard he hung up his guns."

Mort's puzzlement looked to be genuine. Stark was prone to believe he hadn't heard about Garland lurking in the area. Whatever the Kansas outlaw was up to, he seemed to be playing his cards close to his vest.

"Anybody else hiring?" Stark pressed in order to keep up his charade.

"Naw, not to speak of." Mort scowled. "You really looking for work? A high-dollar gun like you?"

"Just keeping my ear to the ground, Mort. Thanks."

Stark left his beer and drifted toward the door, conscious of Mort's little eyes following him. A shifty-looking gunslick watched him uneasily from one of the rickety tables. Word of his interest in Garland might or might not spread. But at least he had a pretense now for looking for the outlaw.

Staying in Corner seemed fruitless. The place had no appeal for him. Mounting, he turned Red away from the hitching rail. Down the alley, the bar girl's victim still snored loudly. Stark put heels to the sorrel. He'd had his fill of this sorry town.

A trail wound through a jungle of cottonwoods and plum thickets to the river's edge. In the gloom the branches appeared as spectral fingers reaching out from the graveyard to claim him. Stark loosened his Colt in its holster. Ghosts or no, the underbrush made a dandy spot for a bushwhacking.

He forded the river without trouble and made camp in a secluded draw where his fire wouldn't be visible to the residents of Corner. Morning found him bellydown on a high ridge, keeping a sharp lookout over the surrounding countryside. Behind him, Red grazed contentedly on the grassy slope below the skyline.

A handful of cowpokes, likely having traveled through the night headed for their notion of a good time, rode out of the Lands and crossed the river to Corner. Stark studied them with his field glasses and made no move to intercept them.

Later in the morning, a lone rider appeared, and Stark looked him over carefully. He saw a short wiry man astride a paint horse that he sat like he'd been born there. The fellow was taking it easy, looking here and there as he rode.

Stark grunted with satisfaction. This yahoo fit the description of Tip Stringer, the cowpoke who'd stumbled onto Dirk Garland's camp. Stringer had arrived right on time for his rendezvous with Stark.

After taking a moment longer to be sure Stringer wasn't being followed, Stark mounted Red and put him down the ridge at an easy lope. Stringer—if that's who he was—spotted him and pulled up to await his approach.

"You Stark?" he drawled, then, eyeing him more closely, added, "Yep, reckon you'd be him, all right."

Stark reined close to shake hands and take stock of the man. Stringer wasn't a kid any longer, and his leathery face was showing the lines and creases that came from long years punching cows in all sorts of weather. His handshake was firm.

"Got word to meet you here," he said affably enough. "Mr. Blaine wants me to show you where I ran into Dirk Garland and his crew." He shook his head ruefully. "Sure wouldn't want to be sitting in your saddle when you go riding into that lion's den, howsomever."

"You certain it was Garland you saw?" Stark put Red into a walk alongside Stringer's black-and-white spotted Indian pony.

"Sure as I'm breathing now," Stringer confirmed. "I seen him back in Kansas in the old days when he was riding high and wide. Big man with a yellow beard and a mane of hair like a palomino stud."

"How'd you run into him in Kansas?"

"Used to work for a little two-cow outfit near Sedalia—an old man and his wife. I was their only hand. Garland and his boys holed up there overnight on occasion. The old couple was too scared of him to say no, even if it would've done any good, which I doubt. I sure wasn't going to object none, neither. All the small-time ranchers and dirt scrabble farmers thereabouts knew Garland was doing a heap of the robbing and killing that was going on, but for the most part he treated them okay, and they looked the other direction when he was passing through. Mainly, he went after banks and trains, and did some cattle rustling on the big spreads."

Stark nodded. The pattern wasn't uncommon. The Dalton Gang still employed similar tactics in the Territory, sometimes relying on small homesteaders for sanctuary and refuge. Such common folk looked on successful outlaws like Bill Dalton and Dirk Garland with a mixture of fear and awe. The outlaw leaders often cultivated their patronage by bestowing generous gifts and favors on them, much to the disgust of the badge-toters sent to track them down.

"Was anything in particular going on that you could see in the camp?"

Stringer shook his head. "Most of the fellows just looked to be loafing around. Like cowpokes marking time before a roundup."

And just what kind of roundup was Garland planning? Stark wondered. "Did Garland have a segundo in the old days?" he asked aloud.

"Reckon that would be Slick Wilson," Stringer answered thoughtfully.

"Slick Wilson," Stark mused. "There's a name I ain't heard in a spell."

"He had a rep as the fastest gun up Kansas way when he was riding with Garland," Stringer recalled. "I seen him practice his draw once when they was staying over, and I don't doubt it for minute." He looked at Stark with curious eyes. "You ever run up against him?"

"If I had, one of us would likely be dead," Stark answered shortly. "Did you see him at Garland's camp in the hills?"

"Naw. Only jasper that stands out in my mind, besides Garland, was a big bruiser who sided Garland. Never seen him before. He was packing a gun, but looked like he was more prone to using his fists. He told Garland I ought to be killed. For a minute I thought old Dirk was going to listen to him." Stringer shuddered. "Look," he said abruptly, "I'll lead you to where I can point you to the camp, but don't go counting on me to get much closer. I think a heap of Mr. Blaine, but he ain't paying me gun wages."

Stark shrugged. "Fair enough."

He continued to press the aging cowhand for details of his encounter with the outlaw chieftain, but learned little more of consequence. He was inclined to put stock in what Stringer said, but it didn't do much to solve the mystery of Garland's presence in the first place.

Stringer proved to be a likable trail companion as they headed deeper into the Indian Lands. Late on the third day, they reined up to watch a steam-belching locomotive rumble across the prairie on a distant rail line.

Stringer shook his head sadly at the sight. "Kind of sorry to see them things come," he commented. "Means it's all going to be changing one day in these parts. Likely to not be any place for your kind or mine, when all the changes are done." He jigged his Indian pony forward before Stark could answer.

He was still moody the next morning when he pulled his horse to a halt and pointed at a pass in the wooded hill country that lay ahead of them.

"Take that pass and head east down the draw," he

began, and launched into the detailed directions of a man who knew the lay of the land.

Stark listened, had him repeat it, then gave a nod of satisfaction. "You didn't spot any lookouts at all?" he asked then.

"Nope. 'Course, there could've been some posted, and I just missed them."

"Are we on Blaine's range here?"

Once more Stringer pointed, this time to the south. "Ten, twelve miles thataway, and you'll be on it. The ranch house is a good thirty miles from here."

"Tell Blaine I'll be in touch, one way or the other. But don't set a timetable. It could be a spell."

"Yessir, I'll tell him." Stringer hesitated, glancing apprehensively at the hills. "Listen, what I said the other day about not getting paid gun wages is true enough, but I don't cotton to a fellow—even the Peacemaker—riding in on Garland and his pack all by his lonesome. I'm willing to go along and side you, if I could be of help."

"Obliged for the offer, Tip." Stark reached to grip his hand. "But, it's my job, not yours. Mr. Blaine *is* paying me gun wages."

Stringer tried to hide the look of relief that touched his weathered face. "Maybe we'll cross trails again," he said gruffly.

"You're a good man to ride with," Stark told him honestly enough. "So long." He wheeled Red around and headed toward the pass in the hills.

Stringer's directions were good, but once Stark was in the hills, he found a convenient gully to hole up in until dusk. If Garland had posted lookouts, there was no point in making their work easy for them.

In the gathering gloom, Stark negotiated the draws and grades of the rugged terrain, senses alert. It was full dark when he left Red ground hitched, donned his

Apache moccasins, and went forward on foot like a wraith, shotgun in hand.

A pale half moon and a host of stars gleamed in the black sky, their wan illumination lost in the shadows of the hills and gullies. The silence of the night was broken only by the whisper of an owl's wings, a raccoon's trill, a wolf's lonely lament. Stark paused often to listen and scent the breeze, detecting nothing to alarm him. No human sound or scent reached him.

He was pretty certain of what he was going to find long before he bellied over the final ridge and gazed down into the blackness of the small valley that had held Dirk Garland's camp. There was no flicker of firelight, no sounds of men or their mounts, no odors of human habitation. The camp was long deserted. Garland and his crew had pulled up stakes, likely spooked by Stringer's discovery of their lair.

Stark returned to Red and made a smokeless camp. With dawn, mounted again, he made his way once more to the site of the camp. Garland had been there, all right, he discerned quickly enough—or at least someone with a score of followers had been holed up in the valley for a spell.

From scattered horse droppings, and the ashes of a campfire that had been crudely covered over with dirt, he calculated they'd been gone for several days. There had been at least one rain shower since their departure, but it would've taken a considerable downpour to obliterate the sign left by a score of men heading farther back into the hills.

Stark struck their trail and stayed with it, cautiously ranging far out to one side so as not to ride into an ambush. Whatever Garland was planning, he didn't want it noised about, and it stood to reason he'd take some precautions besides just moving his camp.

Late in the afternoon, from high up on a wooded hillside, Stark spotted a lone sentry keeping an eye peeled on the trail the riders had followed. On foot, Stark slipped past the lookout's position and prowled on through the evergreens, scrub oaks, and undergrowth clinging to the hillsides.

His nostrils caught the scent of a camp, and he heard a man's voice. Warily he edged forward to the lip of a large grassy draw studded with outcroppings of dark, lichen-covered boulders. He saw a single banked fire with a coffeepot on it. An ancient cabin and a separate lean-to had been erected at some point by earlier squatters. A couple of rough hombres loitered about. A large rope corral had been set up, but only a handful of horses were in it. Stark noted other signs that the camp had once held a large number of men.

Crouching in concealment, he watched, and the truth dawned on him. Garland had moved his camp, right enough, but now it was all but deserted. Leaving only a few hands to guard the site, Garland and most of his gang had ridden out for parts, and purposes, unknown.

Stark chewed on it a bit. He could do a circuit of the camp and pick up the gang's trail, then do his best to follow them to see what they were up to. But that might well result only in a wild goose chase, and accomplish very little. Or he could try to grab one of the remaining gang members and force some kind of explanation from him. But he wasn't partial to such methods, and snatching one of these jaspers would, in the end, only reveal to the others, and maybe Garland himself upon his return, that an enemy was lurking in the vicinity of the camp.

No, Garland hadn't abandoned this hideout completely, and it stood to reason that he'd be coming back. Best to settle down and wait him out, Stark decided. Silently he withdrew from his vantage point and set about looking for a likely spot to hole up until the outlaw returned.

Chapter Five

They were waiting for Prudence when she left her office in the early dusk and headed toward her hotel. Her mind was still busy with details of her strategy for tomorrow's hearing. She heard only a muffled command from the dim alley before three burly figures, kerchiefs masking their faces, erupted out of the gloom and laid rough hands on her. A meaty palm was pressed hard against her lips, stifling her cry.

Fear and outrage made her fight—kicking, stomping, scratching, even trying to strike with her fists as she had seen cowboys do in brawls. It made no difference, other than giving her the satisfaction of a few grunts and curses of pain and surprise. Then her arms were twisted painfully behind her so she doubled forward, and some sort of fabric replaced the hand over her mouth, effectively gagging her. A thong or rope was slipped expertly around her wrists.

"Quit it, missy, or we'll carry you out of here!" a man's guttural tones ordered.

She wasn't ready to quit, but they hustled her deeper into the alley before she could resist further. Shock and panic gripped her heart as tightly as the hard fingers of her captors held her arms.

"Unhand her, you scoundrels, or I'll fire!" The commanding voice from the alley's mouth bounced echoes between the brick walls.

Relief flooded through Prudence. As her abductors slowed in surprise, she had a moment's view over her shoulder of the unmistakable long-haired figure of Temple Houston, poised like a duelist in the mouth of the alley, pistol extended at arm's length.

The next instant a huge form loomed up behind him. Their figures seemed to merge with a flailing of arms. There were more of them, Prudence realized with horror. How many? What did they want? Temple Houston collapsed limply to the ground. Prudence got one last harrowing glimpse of his conqueror looming gigantically over his still form. Struck down from behind, he'd never had a chance.

And her own chances of succor were rapidly vanishing. In moments, following what was obviously a prearranged route, her captors had hustled her away from the main streets and into a much more disreputable part of town. And as they passed, other figures joined them from shadowy doorways and gloomy niches to form a sizable group of masked and armed men. Remotely, beneath her breathless fear, she understood that, just as their accomplice had been stationed so as to waylay Houston, so had other cohorts been positioned strategically to intercept potential trouble and cover their retreat.

Their retreat to where?

She got a partial answer when, minutes later, the entire group reached a stable on the outskirts of town. There, a dozen saddled horses waited. Astride one of them was a striking figure of a man—tall and broad. Dim lantern light from the window of a shed gleamed off pale golden hair that hung to his shoulders. His face was also masked.

He barked low terse commands that had the men stepping quickly to their saddles. Prudence was thrust inelegantly up on one as well. She felt her ankles being bound beneath the barrel of the animal's body.

The golden-maned rider pulled close to her and caught her horse's reins. "Can't sit a sidesaddle the way we're headed," he growled in some sort of absurd apology, then raised his voice. "Everybody accounted for?" Triumph rang in his tones.

"Everyone's here." Another man pushed his horse up beside the leader's, the other riders yielding ground to him.

The blond passed the reins of Prudence's horse to him, then barked, "Let's ride!" and wheeled his horse expertly about.

The lights of Guthrie quickly fell away behind them. They were headed crosscountry, staying clear of the major roads. Prudence found it hard to conceive of the fact that she had literally been snatched off a Guthrie street and whisked away by a mob of riders without a single hitch.

Well, one hitch. Her heart quailed at the thought of Temple Houston, struck down attempting to save her. He must've been just coming from the building in her wake, perhaps trying to catch her and persuade her to join him for dinner once again. Was he still alive? And, if so, what could he do? Trailing her abductors, she guessed, would be all but impossible for even skilled trackers, given the amount of traffic in the Guthrie area. And absolutely no one would have any idea of the direction they had taken.

Her horse was positioned close behind the leader and the other man who seemed to be his lieutenant. She saw he wore an old gun slung low at his side. Humiliation at her unladylike position burned within her, but she knew the relatively minor indignity was liable to be the least of her worries before long.

The leader drew his mask down, but she still couldn't see his face clearly. "Any trouble?" he demanded of his companion. His big body seemed to flow smoothly with the galloping of his steed.

"Some fancy dude threw down on us," Prudence heard the other man's reply. "Shed did for him."

"Dead?" the leader demanded sharply.

"Can't say. You know Shed, though." The last words were fatalistic.

Prudence couldn't tell whether the leonine chieftain was pleased by the report.

She summoned her courage and uttered a wordless protest beneath her gag. Language was her stock in trade. To be deprived of it only added to her sense of helplessness.

The leader cocked his head back in her direction, and his face was revealed for the first time in the faint moonlight. Broad and fleshy, and somehow repellent to her, she knew many women would've found an immoral appeal in it, although he was no longer a young man. A pale beard furred the lower portion of his features.

He slowed his horse so it dropped back beside hers. "Got to leave you trussed up like that a mite longer, Missy McKay." He rolled her name off his tongue as if taking great pleasure in it. "Can't afford to have you trying to hightail it, or sing out for help. But don't you worry your pretty little head. Nothing bad's going to happen to you for the time being." He leered. "Not that my boys, and even myself, wouldn't have some ideas along those lines if things was different. But just now, I need you all in one piece.'' He laughed crudely, then put his horse once more at the head of the pack.

Prudence clung to the saddle horn so tightly her fingers cramped. She barely felt the pain. The wild beating of her heart seemed to drown out the pounding of the horses' hooves as they raced on across the darkened prairie.

He'd give it one more day, Stark decided, then he'd change his strategy. Conditions in the near-deserted hideout had remained the same, and he was growing restless with inaction. Further, the dark notions of the sort of depredations Garland might be committing prodded him like sharp spurs.

He had holed up in a dense thicket near the camp. Avoiding the careless lookouts hadn't been hard, and he'd spent most of the daylight hours observing the hideout. There were five hard cases who'd been left behind as a skeleton crew. Stark felt as though he knew each of them a lot better than he would've ever wanted to under any circumstances.

They took turns standing guard and spent the rest of their time loafing and idling about the camp. They all looked to be experienced fighting men. One lean hawkish hombre spent hours at a time honing the keen blade of his bowie knife or practicing with it against imaginary opponents. After receiving painful slashes on a couple of occasions, his companions had refused to engage in any more mock duels with him. When he'd pressed the issue, one of them had backed him down at gunpoint. A hard crew. Even their games could get deadly.

Watching the knife man now as he feinted and thrust, naked torso gleaming with sweat in the sunlight, Stark had to admit the fellow knew how to handle a big blade. Stark sleeved sweat from his own forehead and automatically reached to touch the wooden hilt of his bowie sheathed at his side.

Faint vibrations reached him through the hard ground where he was stretched on his stomach. A lot of horses headed this way, he realized with a tautening of his muscles. Could be his wait was over.

He unlimbered his field glasses, but didn't lift them to his eyes. In moments a pack of riders spilled into the draw. Stark squinted down at them, then stiffened in shock and whipped the glasses to his eyes.

He recognized the blond Dirk Garland right off from Stringer's description, and from an old Wanted poster he'd seen. But his attention was fixed on the bedraggled feminine form bound astride one of the blowing horses. There was no mistaking the dark hair and small shapely figure of Prudence McKay.

Stark lowered the glasses, stared hard, shook his head, then raised the glasses again. Prudence didn't appear to be hurt, but she slumped in the saddle as though exhausted. Anger drew Stark's mouth into a thin line. While he'd been watching Garland's camp, the outlaw must've been making a raid on Guthrie to abduct Prudence McKay. But why seize the female lawyer? Stark didn't know, but he had a nasty hunch that her being in the camp below had a lot to do with Garland's presence here in the Lands.

He thrust the milling questions to the back of his mind. They could wait. For now, he needed to stop behaving like a greenhorn and pay attention to the men he was going to have to outfight or outwit. For he knew that, regardless of what he was being paid to do, and regardless of the odds, he wasn't going to leave a lady like Prudence McKay in the hands of these savages if he could help it.

First, he focused on Dirk Garland himself as the big outlaw swung down from his saddle. An old hand at the hardcase game, he sized Garland up as one used to giving orders. Stark caught himself trying to read some motive or purpose in the florid, bearded features. It was futile. Resolutely he shifted the glasses to the aging gunhawk who seemed to shadow Garland's every move.

That would be Slick Wilson, he surmised. Rumor had it he'd killed a dozen men in stand-up fights, and a handful more in various squabbles. Wilson still had the lithe, supple moves of a gunman. Stark wondered if he'd lost any of his reputed speed over the years.

Another figure caught his eye. Big and burly, the fellow seemed to dwarf the bay he'd been riding. Stark recollected Stringer's account of riding into the camp and suspected this bruiser was the one who'd urged Garland to do him in.

Careful to keep the glasses shaded so a reflection from the lens would not betray him, he continued to survey the motley pack as they scattered about the campsite. He counted a total of twenty men in all, and he assessed them bleakly as probably the roughest bunch of rogues and desperadoes he'd ever locked horns with.

There was some semblance of order to the way they saw to their horses and set to other routine chores. Garland ran a disciplined camp. That made him and his men even more dangerous.

The outlaw leader stood for a time with his hands on his hips, arrogantly surveying his domain. Then he jerked his head commandingly and strutted away. One of his men, standing nearby, caught Prudence's wrist and led her in Garland's wake. They reached the small lean-to that backed up to a steep wall of the draw.

Briefly Garland addressed the captive. Stark couldn't hear his words, but he was pleased to see Prudence straighten her shoulders and answer assertively. Good; at least he hadn't broken her spirit.

Stark lowered the glasses, conscious he was sweating

more than the heat warranted. As if he had somehow seen Stark's movement, or sensed his presence, Garland suddenly broke off his talk with Prudence and snapped his head about, the pelt of his hair shining gold in the sunlight. For a span of heartbeats his gaze ranged over the area where Stark lay. The Peacemaker stopped breathing, stopped thinking. He did his best to become a part of the grass and brush and rocks that concealed him. Only when Garland turned back to Prudence did Stark draw in a silent breath.

Garland spoke a few more words to Prudence. Abruptly then he reached out and seemed to snatch something—a locket?—from around her neck. She flinched but stood firm. Over her protests, Garland thrust her into the lean-to. Stark had a last glimpse of her frightened, bemused features before Garland shoved the plank door closed and secured it with a rope and peg lock. He left the hard case stationed there as a guard.

Garland summoned another hombre. Stark recognized him as one of the men who'd been left to watch the camp, the one who'd backed down the knife artist. Garland spoke to him for almost five minutes, obviously giving instructions. Several times he pointed emphatically to the north, toward Kansas. He thrust something into the gunslick's hand. Stark remembered the locket, or whatever it was Garland had taken so roughly from his captive. Finally the outlaw chieftain pressed what looked like an envelope on his underling and dismissed him.

Garland continued to keep an eye on him as the fellow hurriedly saddled a fresh horse, then ducked under the overhang where supplies were stored. He emerged with bulging saddlebags and wasted no time in mounting and hightailing it out of camp.

Clearly, Garland had sent him on some sort of mission, Stark mused. Did it have to do with the prisoner?

Some bit of Stark's memory nudged him then with what might've been the answer to the whole puzzle, but the notion slipped away before he could grasp it.

Slick Wilson approached Garland, and the leader issued more orders, turning once to glance searchingly back up at the surrounding terrain. Stark hugged the ground. At last Garland swaggered off to the cabin. He had the air of a man well pleased with himself.

Apparently relaying his chief's orders, Wilson set about dispatching men to what Stark suspected were lookout posts. He was certain Wilson even put a pair of them riding patrol. Careless he might've been at his first hideout, but Garland clearly wasn't taking any chances now. Observing the camp was going to get a sight more hazardous, Stark suspected grimly.

He looked at the lean-to. Prudence seemed safe enough for the time being. Whatever his purpose for abducting her, Garland apparently didn't want her hurt.

Stark scowled darkly. One of the riders had crested the bank of the draw and was meandering in his direction. Although it galled him, he knew he needed to clear out for now and try to devise a plan.

Stealthily he slipped away from the lip of the draw and faded back into the hills.

Chapter Six

When the one she'd heard called Slick Wilson came for her, Prudence was almost relieved. At least it meant a brief respite from the filthy hovel where they had imprisoned her, and where she had spent a near-sleepless night. At best, Wilson's appearance might mean she would finally get some answers as to why she had been brought here.

Her worst fears had abated somewhat over the days spent on the trail with her disreputable captors. While surely not gentlemen, they had, at their chieftain's orders, treated her with some minimal respect. Had there been a chance to escape, she would've taken it, although how she could've hoped to elude them ultimately was beyond her ability to imagine. But no opportunity had presented itself.

Hope of rescue had also faded. Even if Temple Houston had survived Shed's brutal and cowardly assault, there would have been no way for him to put a posse on the trail of her abductors.

She knew the leader was Dirk Garland, and that his men, out of fear or esteem, or maybe both, obeyed his orders with few complaints. And she knew that he had once run with most of these men as an outlaw in Kansas before settling down on a ranch. What had caused him to forsake the ranch was still a mystery. But it was one she hoped she would soon solve.

As best she could, she straightened her clothing as Wilson led her toward the cabin. She had been provided with a small man's jeans and shirt and had donned them eagerly, glad to discard the torn and frayed dress she had worn since her capture. She still felt immodest but was determined to make the best of things.

She winced as she pulled her fingers through her tangled hair. She must look a sight. Her legal training had taught her to always try to look her best when appearing before a judge. And she didn't fool herself. If she was being taken before Garland, then he held more power over her than any judge in a real court had ever held over any defendant she'd ever represented.

Several of the outlaws loitered about. One of them was throwing a bowie knife as big as a small sword at a tree trunk. He ignored her, but she felt the unclean eyes of some of the others on her. None of them spoke audibly, but one man whispered to another, and both laughed. Wilson's head came around sharply, and the mirth was stifled. She fought the flush she could feel wanting to rise to her face. Now, confronted with the boredom of camp life, their restraint might have its limits.

At the rough-hewn door of the cabin, Wilson knocked, then, at a growled response, pushed it open and motioned her in. Despite herself, she hesitated, looking to him for some sign of her fate. His eyes were old and tired, with not much life in them. They told her nothing. Summoning her resolve, she stepped forthrightly past him and entered the cabin. He didn't follow.

She found herself alone with Dirk Garland. He was seated at a lopsided table in a chair that looked too small for his bulk. The remains of a meal were before him. The cabin was neater than she would've expected. The furnishings were crude.

He gestured at the tin dishes. "You hungry?" he demanded.

She was revolted, but tried not to show it. She shook her head. "No." She had been given some bacon and beans earlier. They sat like a cold lump in her stomach.

Garland grunted and leaned back in his chair. He wore a vest of some sort of animal fur that was almost the color of his beard, and without his hat, it was obvious his hairline had receded some. A sheen of grease from his recent meal coated his lips. Watching her, he licked them clean.

"Sit down if you want." He waved a thick arm at the other chair at the table.

Prudence shook her head mutely. Her heart was hammering against her ribs, and she was suddenly afraid she wouldn't be able to draw breath.

"Suit yourself." Garland cocked his shaggy head. "Nobody gave you no trouble last night, did they?"

"No," she said again.

He nodded with satisfaction. "They got orders that no harm's to come to you. Anybody tries anything, I'll let Shed work him over, or I'll kill him myself."

She shouldn't just stand here and let him dictate the conversation, Prudence chided herself. She hadn't gotten to be a successful attorney by being meek and submissive.

"Why am I here?" she asked flatly, and was gratified that her voice held firm.

"That's why I had you brung over to see me," Garland advised. "Figured you needed to know why we snatched you, so you wouldn't go getting any fool notions about escaping."

"Then tell me why," Prudence prompted, careful to keep any note of pleading out of her voice.

"I reckon you know who I am. Dirk Garland. You ever heard of me before?"

"I've heard of you," Prudence said stiffly. The depredations of this man and his gang were notorious back in her home state.

Garland puffed up a little with a repellent pride. "I walked wide and tall through Kansas in the old days," he boasted. "Me and the fellows took what we wanted from the big boys—the railroaders, the bankers, the cattle barons. But we never hurt the little folk none. Always went out of our way to treat them right."

Prudence bit back her acid response to this dubious account of the man's outlaw career. Debating with him wouldn't get her any of the answers she needed right now.

Garland seemed disappointed at her lack of comment. "But things got too civilized, and the big boys started making it hot for us. Their kind owns the lawdogs, you know. Anyway, I could see how the final hand would end up being played, and I knew it was time to cash in our chips. A few of my men didn't want to go along, so I cut them loose. But most of the fellows could see I was right. I bought a big spread—I'd been stashing some of the loot away after every job.

"I took on all the rest of my men as hired hands. We settled down and went straight, by Godfrey, and we made that ranch work! The Bar G. That was our brand. The lawdogs never had nothing on us, so all they could do was sit by and gnash their teeth." Garland smirked at his memories.

The big man's vanity was disgusting. "What does this have to do with me being a prisoner?"

"I'm getting there, girlie. You just hush up and listen, you hear?"

Prudence nodded.

Garland shifted in his chair. "That's better." Unexpectedly he rose to his feet. Prudence shrank back ever so slightly. But Garland only crossed to a sagging shelf, snatched up a bottle of whiskey, and returned to his chair. He pulled the cork with his teeth, opened them to let it drop to the table, then took a double gulp of the amber fluid. "Want a snort?" he offered, thrusting the bottle at her.

Prudence repressed a shudder and shook her head mutely.

"Well, where was I? Yep, me and the boys hung up our guns, so to speak, and took to ranching. I had me a son by that time; name of Nick. His mother was a no-account bar floozy. Pretty little thing, though. Favored you a bit, come to recollect. I never even knew I had the boy until she took sick and died. That's when I got word of it. She and I wasn't married, but I never figured that made no difference. Blood's blood is how I look at it, and that boy's my blood."

Prudence wanted to shake her head in bafflement. Where was her captor headed with this rambling account of his sordid family relationships?

"When I learned about the boy, I got custody of him, legal-like, and brung him out to the Bar G. Got him on his thirteenth birthday. He was a chip off the old block, right enough, even to being a little wild like his pa at that age." Garland nodded with evident satisfaction over his misspent youth.

"I tried to do right by him, tried to keep him from riding down the owlhoot trail like I done. But he had a stubborn streak in him, and, truth to tell, I reckon he felt like I'd done his ma dirty by taking off all them years ago. But shoot, I never even knowed she was in the family way.'' He shrugged as if to dismiss such minor moral concerns.

''He took to running with some hard types—regular lowlifes, the scum of they earth. They corrupted him. That's what they done. Dragged him down with them. Oh, I seen it coming, and I done my best to stop it. I gave him a licking or two to set him straight, but it didn't do no good. Just made him meaner and ornerier, and more determined than ever to go against what I taught him.''

And how many boys like his son had Garland himself corrupted and led down the wrong trail? Prudence reflected with grim irony. Every person made their own choices, but with a role model like his father to emulate, it was no wonder the young Garland had gone bad. And the very real anguish she could read in Garland's eyes told her that he was suffering for the choices his son had made, the very choices he himself must have made as a young man.

But what did any of this have to do with her?

''He got himself in bad trouble,'' Garland continued. ''About the worst there is, I reckon, in the eyes of the law. He and the sorry amateur pack he rode with tried to pull a bank job in some two-bit town. Should've been greenhorn's work. But he got riled and dropped the hammer on some farmer who just happened to be in the bank. Fool thing to do. The kid should've known better.'' Garland sounded outraged at the mess his son had made of being an outlaw.

''Was your son tried for what he did?'' Prudence ventured, still trying to grasp why Garland was interested in her.

''Not yet, he hasn't,'' Garland said with a growl. ''But they're fixing to, soon enough. Yeah, he'll be put on trial before twelve men who were friends of that farmer he killed.''

A glimmer of an idea came to Prudence. ''Mr. Garland,'' she spoke up with the greatest assurance she had felt in days. ''I'm an attorney. I'm quite well versed in criminal matters. I could look into your son's case. I could see to it that he gets a fair trial.''

Garland spat. ''Don't want no fair trial; that'll just get my son hanged. And I don't need no lady shyster handling his case. I got a good attorney looking after that end of things.''

''Well then, you've done everything you can for your son.'' Prudence used her best persuasive tones. ''No one could ask for more than that.''

Garland waved the hand that still grasped the whiskey bottle. ''It ain't enough! His lawyer already done told me that Nick don't have the chance of a rabbit in a wolf pack. They got him held so there's no chance of busting him out. He'll be convicted and sentenced to hang.''

''There may be mitigating circumstances—'' Prudence began.

''I'll not have my boy hanged!'' Garland slammed the bottle down on the table. Whiskey sloshed out of it, and the rickety table shook beneath the impact. Garland's lips were peeled back until he resembled a lion indeed.

Prudence recoiled. ''But what can I do about it?'' she stammered.

''You can't do nothing,'' Garland told her. ''Nothing, that is, except maybe make Judge Uriah McKay see things a little different when the time comes for trial.''

''My father!'' Prudence breathed wonderingly. ''He's the judge who is trying your son's case, isn't he?''

''Blamed straight he is,'' Garland said with savage glee. ''And now that I got you, I can make him dance to whatever tune I fiddle!''

"That's why you kidnapped me? To . . . to force my father to release your son?"

Garland's grin was wicked. "That's right, hon. I got me a man headed up Kansas way right now to contact him. He has a letter telling your daddy what I want him to do, and what's going to happen to his little girl if he don't. And he's carrying that locket of yours, so the judge won't think I'm just funning him."

"It won't work!" Prudence protested. "Father would never—" She broke off in midsentence. What would her father do? His stern commitment to the law would never permit him to unjustly dismiss a case. But she also knew that the idea of hurt coming to her would be all but intolerable to him when he had the power to prevent it. For a moment, concern over her own fate gave way to a biting distress over the terrible dilemma her father would soon have to confront.

"It's real simple," Garland taunted brutally. "If my son hangs, why, then so do you."

"My father won't give in," she said with more conviction than she actually felt. "There will be people looking for me. My father will see to that. And I'll be missed in Guthrie. Posses will be sent out. Federal troops will be called in!"

Garland sneered. "You think they could run me to ground? It's been tried before, sweetheart, back in my outlaw days. I was never caught. I told you, I quit the owlhoot trail on my own. What makes you think it'd be any different now?"

"They'll take your messenger into custody. He'll be forced to talk. He'll lead them back here!"

"I done thought of that," Garland spoke with utter confidence. "I got it arranged so he won't never make personal contact with your pa. And, even if he does get caught, I've made it real clear in my letter what'll happen to you if he don't get back here on schedule. You'd still be alive, but you wouldn't be in the same condition you're in now!''

A chill horror gripped her. She forced her mind to work, to analyze this bizarre situation as though she were in a courtroom. All she had left was bluff. "My father doesn't have the authority to release your son. He can't simply take it upon himself to do that. It wouldn't be permitted.''

"I figure your pa could manage it, one way or the other if your life depended on it. I ain't too concerned with what it does to his standing in the community.''

Garland was no fool, she conceded to herself. He'd put a lot of scheming into his devilish plan. She felt a terrible frustration at being a pawn in his crude hands.

"You're risking your ranch," she tried a new strategy. "Even if you're successful in getting your son freed, you'll be on the run all over again—a hunted man. You'll lose everything you've achieved since you gave up being an outlaw.''

Something feral and cunning flashed in his eyes. "I figure it'd be worth it to have my boy set free," he said more casually than he'd spoken since she'd entered the cabin. "I've made my way as an outlaw before. I reckon I can do it again, especially if I got Nick siding me.''

The awful truth of his plans for her came to Prudence as a sudden conviction. "What about me?" she asked without a quaver. "If my father releases your son, will I be freed?''

" 'Course you would. I'm a man of my word.''

Prudence could see the lie in the hard glint of his yellow eyes, the flare of his wide nostrils, the faint lifting of his thick lips. No matter what her father did, Garland planned to kill her, she understood with bleak certainty. He couldn't leave her behind as a witness. The only reason he had kept her alive up until now was as insurance in case he was somehow forced to produce further proof that he held her captive. It was likely he had even developed some scheme so that his name wasn't connected to the extortion threat. In the end, he planned on getting both his son and his ranch back.

"You see, honey? I got your pa herded into a box canyon. Ain't no way out for him or you, unless he cooperates."

"How did you find me?" she asked to give herself time to think.

"Shoot, everybody knows how proud the judge is of his daughter, the lady lawyer in Oklahoma Territory. He's always bragging on you. It was easy enough to have one of my men keep an eye on you in Guthrie and report back to me, so's I could plan how to snatch you."

Prudence swallowed hard. This was no courtroom where her skill at debate and her knowledge of the law could win her freedom, she realized dismally. Garland stood as her judge and jury, and, she was convinced, when he had no more need of her, as her executioner. His obsession with his son's freedom would brook no interference from any objections she could raise. She felt her shoulders sag. Case dismissed. No court of higher appeal.

"Just so you know how things stand," Garland spoke with a triumphant tone that told her he had read her acceptance of defeat. "You'll be kept safe, like I done told you. Don't give me no trouble, and I won't go hard on you. Wouldn't want no harm to come to my prize filly, now would I?"

Beaten, Prudence took refuge in Scripture, which, after all, was the final law. " 'The Lord preserveth all them that love him,' " she quoted. " 'But all the wicked will he destroy.' "

Garland blanched, then snorted with contempt. "He ain't done it yet, girl, and I been mighty wicked in me day!'' He laughed uproariously, then bellowed for his lieutenent to take her out.

Shoulders squared, her spirit in tatters, she didn't resist Wilson's grasp on her elbow as he guided her from the room.

The sunlight was a relief after the dimness of the cabin and the evil of its occupant. Wilson released his light hold on her arm, and it dawned on her that, for an instant, at any rate, she was free. To submit further to her captors, to allow herself to be placed once more in the shed, would only lessen her chances of ever making good her escape. She might never have a better opportunity than right at this moment.

Meekly she let her warden herd her toward the hovel while her eyes raced over the camp. Several of the outlaws were still loafing about, but they weren't paying so much attention to her as they had on her first appearance that morning. The rope corral was not far away. If she could reach there, get astride a horse, she was a good enough rider that, even bareback, she might manage to win free of the hideout. After that, she could attempt to elude pursuit in the woods and underbrush.

There was no time to analyze her frail plan. Without warning, she sprinted for the rope corral. Behind her, she heard Wilson's angry curse, then the pound of his feet in her wake. Yells sounded from some of the other outlaws. Desperately she strained to reach the corral, and she fancied Wilson's footsteps were falling behind. The path was clear ahead of her.

Then, from out of nowhere it seemed, the mountainous form of the man known as Shed loomed suddenly in front of her. She tried to swerve, but one long arm enfolded her. Laughing with crude enjoyment, he hugged her to his foul chest.

Her struggles were useless. He literally swept her clear of the ground. She felt his great arms crushing the breath from her. The stench of him was in her nostrils. His laughter echoed in her ears.

"Put her down, Shed!" Wilson's voice cracked across her awareness.

From the corner of her vision she caught sight of the gunfighter. His chest was heaving from the sudden exertion of the short chase, but the gun he held aimed at Shed's skull was as steady as a steel bar.

Shed's laughter died. He turned to stare at the older man. Prudence felt like a doll in his grasp. "I ain't hurting her none," he protested, then set her carefully back on her feet, keeping his eyes on Wilson the whole time.

Holstering his gun, Wilson stepped forward and snared her wrist before she could catch her balance. His grip was like iron. "Don't try that again." He gave her arm a painful wrench. "You understand?"

Prudence nodded contritely. After the embrace of Shed, the filthy hovel didn't seem uninviting.

"Put some bracelets on her, Slick," ordered the voice of Dirk Garland. The big blond man had emerged from the cabin to survey the scene with blazing eyes. He strode forward and jabbed a stiffened finger against Wilson's chest. "And don't let her get loose again, Savvy?"

Wilson's eyes were dangerous, but he nodded. "Yeah, I savvy."

Garland wheeled away. "Good job stopping her," he addressed Shed. "But I won't have her manhandled." He lifted his voice in a commanding shout. "You men, listen up! Any man lets her escape, any man who mistreats her, I'll hang him myself!"

Prudence saw from the faces of the outlaws that they didn't doubt him for a minute. She didn't doubt him either. Her spirit wilted as she felt the cold steel of handcuffs being snapped around her slender wrists. It didn't appear likely that she'd be given another opportunity to make an escape. She had lost the only real chance she was going to have.

Unprotesting, she let herself be thrust back into the darkness of the shed.

Chapter Seven

Lever-action shotgun across his saddle, Stark rode boldly into the outlaw camp. He kept his eyes moving, watching the startled reactions of the hard cases as they spied him. None of them hauled iron, but more than one tensed hand hovered near a holstered pistol.

Stark knew he was wading barefoot into a creekful of water moccasins, but, after chewing things over, he hadn't been able to see a route around it. He had to rescue Prudence, and he still needed to know what Garland was doing here. No doubt, Prudence's abduction was part of it, but with her at risk in Garland's hands, he couldn't afford to wait and watch in hopes of figuring it all out. The time had come to take the bull by the horns.

The big bruiser he'd noted earlier strode in front of his horse and halted, fists on his hips. He was built like a buffalo and bore the scars of battles with other bulls.

"Who the deuce are you?" he demanded as Stark reined to a stop.

"I'm here to see Garland."

"That still don't tell me who you are, pilgrim."

Others of the owlhoots were drawing closer. Stark waited until they were in earshot. "The name is James Stark," he said evenly.

There was murmur among the gathered outlaws. The big man scowled. "That doesn't buy you nothing here."

"Don't it?" Stark drawled. "Call your boss or step aside, and we'll see."

"Haw!" the bruiser snorted derisively, and reached for Red's bridle.

Stark twitched the reins, and the sorrel stud stepped delicately backward out of reach. Caught off balance, the big yahoo lurched forward. He straightened, and Stark wondered briefly if he meant to tackle both horse and rider barehanded.

"Ease up, Shed."

The speaker was the middle-aged gunman Stark had pegged as Slick Wilson. He paced forward with deceptive laziness of a lobo wolf, head cocked a little as he regarded Stark. His right hand hung near the butt of his old pistol. Stark got the impression he'd been watching from among the ranks of outlaws, biding his time before stepping forward. He chided himself for not spotting the aging shootist before now.

Wilson stopped far enough back from Stark's mounted form so that he would only have to draw his gun and tilt it a little from waist level to line it with Stark's chest, if it came to gunplay.

"You the one they call the Peacemaker?"

Stark's mouth quirked in a slight grin. "Been called worse."

Wilson's lips twitched. "Ain't we all?" he agreed laconically. "Even up north we've heard of you."

"You'd be Wilson."

A dark pride formed in Wilson's flat, killer's eyes. "Yeah, I'm Wilson. Not many of our breed left, these days."

"Not many of our caliber, anyway," Stark assented.

A restless curiosity had replaced the gleam of pride in Wilson's gaze. "Step down," he invited with an easy gesture of his left hand. His right—his gunhand—didn't move.

Deliberately Stark slid the shotgun into its sheath, lifted a leg over the horn, and slipped out of the saddle, facing Wilson the whole time. His own hand didn't stray too far from the butt of the Colt Peacemaker. Wilson watched his every move.

Without looking about, Stark could sense the tension dancing along the nerves of the watching owlhoots. It was doing some dancing along his own, as well.

"What wind blows you to these parts?" Wilson asked lazily.

"A cold, hungry one."

Wilson cocked a graying eyebrow. "Meaning?"

Stark shrugged. "You said it yourself. Not many of our kind left. Jobs are few and far between."

"You're looking for work?" Wilson demanded skeptically.

Stark hitched his shoulders. "I'd earn my keep."

"I don't doubt it," Wilson murmured dryly. He raised his voice, "Toby, go tell Dirk that the Peacemaker himself is looking to ride the trail with us." One of the watching hard cases hurried for the cabin. "Reckon the boss man will want to hear this," Wilson explained to Stark.

They waited. Stark found his eyes wanting to stray to the lean-to where he knew Prudence was imprisoned. Had she seen him ride in? Was she watching the tense byplay? He corralled his thoughts. Fool thing to be wondering about now.

Dirk Garland emerged from the cabin and strode toward them, the hard case Toby trotting at his heels. The giant, Shed, made way for him as he drew near. He halted and appraised Stark with seeming satisfaction.

"So, you're the Peacemaker," he mused aloud. "Top dog of the hired guns."

Stark saw Wilson's face go tense at his boss's words, but the gunhawk didn't speak.

"I'm Stark."

"And you came to me," Garland said with even more evident satisfaction. He turned on his heel toward the cabin. "I think we ought to have a confab inside. Slick, you and Shed come along." He didn't look back to see if he was obeyed.

Stark took Red's reins and followed, flanked by the two owlhoots. Shed bulked huge beside him. Wilson's face was like old leather now, showing no expression.

"Sit down," Garland ordered Stark once they were in the cabin. He himself dropped into a rickety chair that creaked beneath his weight.

Stark swung a chair away from the table so he could keep an eye on Wilson. The gunman smiled thinly as he saw the move, but his gaze was hooded. He leaned his shoulders against the wall near the door, right hand clasping his left wrist loosely in front of the buckle of his gunbelt. Shed brooded menacingly in a corner.

"I got lookouts posted," Garland commented, eyeing Stark. "What happened so you could ride in here unannounced, bold as brass?"

"I didn't let them see me."

Garland shook his head. "You must be good. Some of them boys stood lookout for me back in the old days, and nobody ever snuck up on my camp."

"Figured to show you that you could use some quality

help.'' Stark kept the edge of his vision on Wilson as he spoke. He might be muscling in on the segundo's territory a little bit here.

"I can always use a top fighting hand," Garland admitted, "Especially these days. And especially if I can trust him."

Stark shrugged. "Show me the color of your money. My trust is for sale, but it don't come cheap."

Garland chuckled down in his deep chest. "So I've heard." His laughter died. "How'd you learn we were out here?"

"Word gets around. I heard tell you'd flown the coop up in Kansas and had come to these parts, but nobody seems to know just why."

"You'll find out why when I'm sure I trust you to cover my back."

"I told you where I stand."

"Yeah. Yeah, I like that. No question of your loyalty so long as the dollar count is right. One thing puzzles me, though."

Scorpions crawled up Stark's spine. "What's that?"

"I always heard you sold your gun, but I ain't never heard tell of you stepping outside the law. Word is, you're in cahoots with the lawdogs in these parts."

"I'm in cahoots with whoever's paying me. There's lots of things you ain't heard—lots of things nobody's heard, because I didn't want them noised about, and I took steps to keep them quiet. So long as the lawmen think I'm working their side of the street, they go easy on me, give me pretty much a free rein. Sometimes they even send business my way. Makes the trail a lot smoother when Evett Nix and his deputies ain't breathing down my neck or snapping at my heels. I even throw them a bone sometimes to keep them happy."

Garland nodded thoughtfully.

"You as good as they say?" Wilson interjected.

Stark shifted his full attention to him. "You ought to know the answer to that. A man with a rep only stays alive as long as he can live up to it."

Wilson's eyes narrowed. "Maybe," he muttered.

"I like the idea of the Peacemaker riding under my brand," Garland announced. "I've had good men riding for me ever since I first saddled up and hit the outlaw trail. Good fighting men—some of the best. They knew I'd side them when the chips were down, knew I'd treat them right when it came time to divvy up. And they knew I could pull a gun or throw a punch with the best of them. I've proved it more than once when I had to." He stroked the tawny fur vest he wore. "You see this? It's the hide of a cougar. Killed him with my knife when he jumped me. Good men will follow an hombre who can do something like that!"

"I'll follow you," Stark said. "Times are getting lean for a man who makes a living by his gun. I figure you're riding herd on something big, or you wouldn't be here. I want a piece of it."

"I can use you, right enough," Garland assured him. "Not that I ain't already got good men under my brand. Take Wilson there. You've heard of him. I reckon he'd be a right fair match for you, even though he's past his prime. But he's still one of the best. He's been with me since the old days. You can't buy loyalty like that!"

Stark cut a glance at Wilson. As he'd expected, the gunman didn't take to being called past his prime. But Wilson handled it stolidly.

"What do you think, Slick?" Garland addressed him. "You figure we can use the Peacemaker?"

Wilson pushed away from the wall and let his hands dangle clear before he answered. "We don't need him," he advised flatly. "And no matter what he says, joining up with us ain't his style. I say, let him drift."

"Let me have the word, boss, and I'll give him some

peace he won't forget anytime soon!" Shed offered eagerly. He clenched one big hand into a massive scarred fist.

"You hear that, Stark?" Garland prodded. "They don't cotton to you riding with us. But they'll do what I tell them. That's the kind of boys I have!"

"You let them make your decisions for you?" Stark inquired coolly.

Garland's florid face flushed even redder. "I make my own decisions!" he snapped. "And I say you'll sign on with us."

"Good enough." Stark made to rise.

"Don't get yourself in a lather. I ain't sure but that there's something in what Slick says. I don't quite trust you myself. Until I do, we're going to have a few rules."

"Such as?" Stark asked coldly.

"First off, you'll answer to Slick, as well as to me. Wouldn't want him to go getting jealous of a new fast gun." Garland laughed as if, to him, the notion of Wilson getting jealous wasn't a serious one.

But it was serious enough to Wilson, Stark sensed. Garland was so busy patting himself on the back that he wasn't reading his own segundo right, much less his newest recruit.

"What else?" Stark prompted.

"I think we'll put you on probation for a spell, just until I'm sure of you. That means you'll be turning your hogleg over to Wilson."

He was being tested, Stark understood. Maybe Garland wasn't as much of a fool as he acted. Could be that the outlaw chieftain had mistrusted Stark's motives from the first, and just wanted to keep him corralled until he could figure Stark's angle.

Wilson stepped forward, left hand extended. "Come on, Stark; let's have it."

He had no choice, Stark calculated, although his in-

stincts screamed against it. Moving carefully, he palmed
the Colt and offered it to Wilson buttfirst. At the last
moment, the inbred reflexes of a fighting man almost
made him twirl the gun to put Wilson under its barrel.
Only the thought of Prudence McKay, held helpless as
a captive, stilled the violent impulse.

Wilson gave a feral grin as he accepted the Colt, as
though he'd read the struggle in Stark's eyes. "You
packing a hideout gun?"

"You think I'd need one?" Stark growled.

Wilson paused, then stuck the Colt in his belt. "Hand
over the knife."

"Let him keep his pigsticker," Garland commanded.
"I wouldn't leave even the Peacemaker unarmed among
this pack of cutthroats." He laughed.

"What about my horse?" Stark asked.

Garland nodded at Wilson. "Put it with the rest of the
stock, and give him his gear. Just hang onto any shooting
irons you come across."

Stark made a mental note to keep track of his guns.
Even with his bowie and the hideout .38, he was starting
to feel a mite undressed.

"You have the run of the camp, but no further,
Stark," Garland instructed him. "And I think I'll have
Shed here keep an eye on you—make sure you stay out
of trouble. You can do that, can't you, Shed?"

The bruiser bared square yellow teeth. One of the
front ones was missing—knocked out, Stark figured, in
some old brawl. "I'll ride herd on him real good, boss."

"I don't need a nursemaid," Stark said coldly. If this
went much further, he'd be near as much a prisoner as
Prudence McKay. "Your boy gets in my way, or tries
to roust me, I'll run over him like a stampede."

Shed rumbled and took a half-step forward before
Garland waved him back. "I wouldn't advise tangling

with Shed. I seen him come close to killing a prizefighter once in a street brawl.''

"Just giving fair warning." Stark met the outlaw's pale golden eyes.

Garland didn't look away, but he spoke to his pet brawler. "Cut him some slack, Shed. Don't go making trouble. You understand?''

Shed grunted an unhappy acknowledgment. Stark shifted his eyes from those of Garland. He hoped he'd gained a little room to maneuver.

Unexpectedly Garland grinned. "I like you, Stark. I think we're cut from the same tough cloth. We both got fire and nails inside us. We'll have to swap tales one of these days.''

"Obliged for taking me on," Stark said wryly.

Garland chuckled like gravel rattling in a pail. "I'll see I get my money's worth. We'll talk about your wages when your probation's over.''

"Make it soon. I'm an impatient man.''

"You won't have no regrets," Garland promised. "Shed, go with him.''

Stark pushed his chair back and rose. He'd gained admission to the enemy camp, but he didn't know if it was going to do him much good. He was still a long ways from freeing Prudence, and he didn't know how much time he had before things reached the boiling point.

Once his gear—minus the shotgun—was stored, he glanced around at Shed, who had stayed on his heels like a suspicious hound. "I figure on taking a look around. You follow along if you want.''

Shed did just that. Stark prowled the hideout, learning its boundaries, appraising Garland's boys. His estimate of them didn't change. They were a hard-riding bunch, maybe gone a little soft from living on a ranch the last few years, but still not a crew to tangle with if a man could take another trail.

Some of the desperadoes knew of his rep and wanted no dealings with him, which suited Stark fine. Blade Nickle was different. He was the lean knife artist Stark had seen while Garland and most of his pack had been absent snatching Prudence.

"Another new man, huh?" Nickle said gaugingly when they met. "There's a few of us didn't ride with Garland in the old days, Stark. Reckon we have to prove ourselves as the new boys." He nodded at Stark's sheathed bowie. "You any good with that?"

"Just use it for whittling and cutting bacon."

A few of the other men looking on laughed uneasily. Knives made most gunslicks nervous. Something about getting cut seemed a whole lot worse than getting shot.

"Yeah, I'll bet that's all you use it for," Nickle spoke with ugly amusement. "No fancy hilt, and it sure wasn't made in some European factory. Appears to me, that's a fighting knife. Like this." His own blade appeared as if by sleight of hand, and he twirled it deftly.

Stark's eyes narrowed at the thin brass inlay along the back of the twelve-inch blade. Several nicks showed in the brass, evidence of the inlay having been used, as it was intended, to trap an opponent's blade when it cut into the soft metal. Nickle was packing a fighting blade himself.

"Let's see it." Stark stuck out his hand.

Nickle snatched the knife back close to his chest. "Nope. Nobody touches my blade but me."

Stark withdrew his hand, studying Nickle a little closer. He was younger than he'd appeared from a distance. His wedge-shaped face was unlined. Across the back of his left hand was the white line of an ugly scar. It was the sort of wound a man was likely to take when he was using his left hand and arm to guard his midriff against an opposing knife. Despite his youth, Blade Nickle didn't look to be very young in experience.

"Maybe we can set up some targets and show these gunslicks how a man chucks a knife, Stark," Nickle suggested. His tone was friendly, but his eyes held a challenge as cold as the blade of his bowie.

"Keep it honed," Stark suggested casually, and drifted off, Shed lumbering behind him.

"Ain't you seen enough of this place by now?" the brawler complained when they'd completed a circuit of the hideout.

"Pack it in if you like," Stark said over his shoulder. He'd been hoping Shed would grow bored and leave him to his own devices, but the brawler evidently took his task seriously.

Deliberately Stark had left the lean-to until last. He ambled in that direction.

"Don't go poking your nose over there," Shed rumbled a warning from behind.

Stark ignored him. He needed to get a closer look at Prudence's prison before he could make plans to bust her out. He'd covered a half-dozen strides when the suddenly heavier thudding of Shed's boots warned him. He did a little bobbing duck and weave so that Shed's reaching fingers slipped off his shoulder before they could tighten. Stark lengthened his stride. Shed grunted in exasperation and caught up with him as he strolled up to the lean-to.

The guard was seated on the ground, leaning back against the wall of the shed. He had tattered, greasy cards spread out in a hand of solitaire on the dirt in front of him.

"This is off-limits, pal," he said without getting up.

"Some kind of lockup, is it?" Stark asked.

"Ain't none of your concern," Shed told him.

"Always like to know where the hoosegow is," Stark drawled.

"Get lost," the card player said in a growl. He tilted his head to gaze up at Shed's imposing height. "Tell Garland I need to be relieved. I been out here all day. I'm getting so bored, I'm liable to start playing my cards honest."

There was no sign of life from within the hovel. Stark studied it surreptitiously as he let himself be herded away by Shed. There were no windows, but the clay-caulked logs that made up the walls showed numerous chinks. A distance of about a yard separated the rear wall from the sheer bank of the draw.

He hadn't seen as much as he'd wanted, but it was going to have to be enough, Stark concluded darkly. Guarded, all but a prisoner, he didn't have the foggiest notion how he was going to get Prudence or himself out of this den of rattlers alive.

Chapter Eight

Nearby, Shed was snoring like a rutting hog, and the camp was cloaked in darkness, when Stark eased out of his bedroll and sat for a moment, testing the night with his senses. He had pretended to doze while waiting for Shed to fall asleep. The brawler seemed to have few friends among his outlaw brethren, so they hadn't been disturbed at the isolated spot where Stark spread his bedroll. Shed had curled up on a tattered blanket like some wild beast.

There were other sleeping forms scattered about. A trio of the owlhoots had shared a bottle until they passed out where they sat. Stark was sure there were guards posted outside the camp, but he could detect none of them patrolling within it. A light breeze whispered down the draw.

Stealthily he eased to his feet. He could always say he was visiting the latrine as an excuse for being up, but it would be better if he wasn't spotted at all. Staying to

the deeper patches of darkness, wishing he'd had the
chance to don his Apache moccasins, he slipped down
the draw toward the lean-to. None of the sleepers stirred
as he passed them.

In the shadow of the sheer wall of the draw, he paused
to reconnoiter. Despite his request of Shed, the surly
solitaire-playing guard at the shed hadn't been replaced,
he noted with satisfaction. The outlaw had moved out
a-ways from the lean-to, but he was still dealing cards
in the small pool of light cast by a flickering lantern.
Stark wondered if he'd started playing honest yet. After
this long at his post, he'd be groggy, and the lantern
would've destroyed his night vision.

Stark observed him for a moment, hoping he'd go
ahead and doze off, but the hard case continued his des-
ultory card game. At last, placing his feet carefully in
the darkness, Stark paced along the base of the gully's
wall until he could slip behind the shed and crouch in
the narrow space there. It was dark as the belly of Jon-
ah's whale.

He waited for his heart to settle down. Borne by the
breeze, the faint odors of the camp's waste, and the
fresher scent of the woodlands beyond touched his nostrils. From back in the hills a coyote yapped.

By feel, he located a chink in the log wall, then used
the point of his bowie to scrape softly at what remained
of the caulking. He paused and strained his ears, imagining he heard a faint rustle from within.

He brought his lips close to the wood and spoke in a
whisper, "Prudence. Can you hear me?"

He was sure his ears caught a sharply indrawn breath.
She must've been lying awake, alone and terrified in her
prison. "Quiet!" he hissed. "I'm just outside the rear
wall. Get as close as you can."

The faint rustle of her movement made him stiffen, as
though she might be overheard. He forced himself to

relax. His nerves, strung taut as a bowstring, were magnifying the sounds that reached his ears, he realized.

He heard her timorous breathing just beyond the wall. Her lips must be only inches from his. "Who . . . who is it?" came her whispered voice.

"James Stark. I'm here to help you."

"Oh, thank God!" She gasped reverently. "I saw you ride in, but I didn't know why you were here. I . . . I thought maybe you were one of them!"

"Shhh," Stark hushed her, although, with the cover of the breeze, their whispered conversation wouldn't be audible over a few feet away. "I had to pretend to join them to get into their camp. Have you been hurt?"

"No," she answered, and now it was Stark who breathed a prayer of thanks. "I tried to escape," she went on with anger and frustration in her tones, "But they caught me."

That resolute spirit of hers still hadn't been broken, Stark noted. He cringed at the thought of her in the hands of men like Garland and Shed. "Can you ride?"

"Yes!" she asserted fiercely.

"Okay. Get some sleep. We won't try anything tonight. I have to work out a plan. May not be able to talk to you again, so try to be ready to go at a moment's notice, night or day."

"I'll be ready," she promised. "But can't you just let me out of here now? We could sneak away in the dark."

"Not yet."

He heard her draw in her breath with frustration. "Please hurry. "They want to use me to force my father to release Garland's son."

Stark chewed it over. It was the kind of barbaric scheme that would appeal to Garland.

"We've got to get word to my father that I'm all right!"

"Don't be impatient," Stark cautioned. "Wait for my move."

Another sigh sounded, this one of resignation. "I'll wait."

Shaking his head at her willfulness, Stark eased back from the wall of the shed.

"What the deuce are you still doing here?" Dirk Garland's voice demanded from out front.

"Nobody relieved me, Boss," came the reply of the guard.

Stark closed his eyes and then opened them. He made himself remain rigid, praying Prudence wouldn't somehow betray his presence. Garland must've been prowling the hideout, maybe to check on his prisoner, when he saw the long-suffering guard.

"Any trouble?" he demanded now of his underling.

"Naw, no trouble." Stark heard the fellow stifle a yawn.

"Go roust one of the other boys to take your place," Garland ordered. "I'll tell Slick to make certain this don't happen again."

"Sure, Boss." The guard moved off, then there was silence.

What was Garland doing? Stark pondered uneasily. Suppose his next step was to check on Stark? If he found the empty bedroll, there'd be the devil to pay.

His mouth a thin hard line, Stark dared to peek around the corner of the lean-to. Rocking on his heels, arms folded across his chest, the outlaw chieftain stood just outside the pool of light cast by the lantern. Its flickering glow glinted gold off his beard and long shock of hair. Stark was reminded of a lion standing watch over its kill.

From back toward the main part of the encampment came the guard's surly tones rousing some luckless comrade. Stark's heart beat faster. If the commotion disturbed Shed, then the big brawler was certain to notice Stark's empty bedding and raise a ruckus.

Stark sank down on his belly and slipped like a snake out from behind the lean-to. The risks of staying put had been outweighed by the risks of his absence being discovered. He inched and wriggled his way forward, the faint scuffling of his passage sounding thunderous in his ears. If Garland spotted him and threw down on his prone form, he wouldn't have a chance of evading the outlaw's aim. He did some more praying as he writhed along the ground in the cloaking darkness.

He made twenty feet, then thirty, before rising up into a crouch. No warning cry sounded. No gunshots exploded. Stark catfooted toward his bedroll. Another man's groggy voice sounded. Stark crossed the last few yards and dropped silently onto his bedding, just as Shed stirred, grunted, rolled over, then sat up.

"What's that blamed racket?" he groused.

Stark sat up himself, shaking his head as if just coming awake. "You say something?" he asked in surly tones.

Shed's blocky head swung around toward him. In the gloom the outlaw was just a hulking silhouette. "What are you up to, Stark?"

"I was sleeping till you woke me. You always carry on like this at night?"

Shed cursed him in anger. "You just watch your step, hombre," he rumbled. "I'm keeping a close eye on you. Don't forget it."

"It'll give me nightmares," Stark said laconically, and settled back down in his blankets.

Shed cursed again, called out an inquiry to the camp at large, then finally curled up once more and started to snore.

It was a spell before Stark could work his way back into slumber.

Shed was still snoring when Stark awoke with first light, but the big guardian roused quickly enough as the camp began to bestir itself. New lookouts rode out to replace those returning after the night shift. A cook fire was started, and Stark joined the group of men gathering there. Shed tagged along, taking some ribbing from his cohorts at his appointed job as watchdog. While a sullen glower from the brawler was enough to silence most comments, Stark noted the angry red flush rising up Shed's bull neck. Shed moved away, but kept an angry glare fixed on Stark as they chowed down on bacon and biscuits.

Other than keeping a wary eye on his whereabouts, Stark ignored Shed. He listened to the crude banter exchanged by the hardbitten owlhoots. It wasn't hard to learn that his Colt and his shotgun were with Slick Wilson's gear under the overhang where the segundo spread his bedroll. Stark noted Wilson having a confab with the night lookouts, likely taking their reports. Garland didn't show himself.

His meal finished, Stark used the dirt of the gully floor to scour the grease from his hands. He slapped the dust off his palms and cast an eye about for Shed. He spotted his jailer engaged in earnest conversation with Blade Nickle. The knife artist was fingering the blade of his bowie. Once he glanced in Stark's direction.

Garland himself and Wilson rode out of camp a while later. Stark guessed they were taking a look-see of their own to make sure the guards were doing their jobs. The outlaw leader spared barely a glance for Stark where he sat crosslegged in the shade of the bank of the draw. Stark watched them go, wondering if this was a daily ritual with them.

"Hey, Stark!" came a jeering call.

Stark swiveled his head about. Blade Nickle was sauntering over to him. Stark stayed seated. "Yeah?"

Nickle stopped about a yard short of him. Under the brim of his hat, his wedge-shaped face was in shadow. "Got an idea for some fun," he proposed.

Stark remembered the bloody games Nickle had played with the other outlaws left behind to look after the hideout. "Not interested," he said.

"Shoot, you ain't even heard my idea yet!"

"Don't need to. I ain't interested."

Nickle's voice turned colder. "You're fixing to hear it anyway. Folks say you're pretty good with a knife. That true?"

"I told you, whittling and bacon."

Nickle chortled. "Well, I got something better than that. Here's what I propose: you and me make a few passes with the blades. Nothing serious. Just a game. First blood wins."

"I'm not much for games."

Nickle cocked his head arrogantly. "You saying you ain't got the nerve to face me?"

"I'm saying I ain't interested." Stark felt a rising edge of anger. He didn't need this sort of trouble. Odds were, no matter what the outcome of Nickle's game, it would only make Stark's position here more precarious. He had a good notion that Garland wouldn't look too fondly on having his men slice each other up in play.

Nickle sighed heavily. "That's mighty disappointing. The fellows are hoping for a little entertainment."

Stark looked past him to where some of the other outlaws were gathering to watch the confrontation. He spotted Shed's burly form and wicked gap-toothed grin among them. He figured the brawler was using Nickle to get his revenge for the ribbing he apparently blamed on Stark. It showed a streak of animal cunning Stark hadn't expected.

"Guess they'll have to be disappointed," Stark said lazily.

"You guess wrong!" Nickle snarled and swung a booted foot in a contemptuous kick at Stark's shoulder.

It never landed. Stark's left arm swept around. His cupped hand caught Nickle's bootheel and spun him away in a half-circle. Stark used the thrust of his arm as leverage to coil to his feet, his right hand plucking his own bowie from leather. An expectant murmur arose from the watchers.

Nickle caught his balance and wheeled, a snarl of rage twisting his face. It widened into a grin as he saw Stark on his feet. His eyes flicked to the bared bowie and the brass inlay along the back of Stark's blade. "I knew that was a fighting knife!" His bowie winked into his hand.

"Careful you ain't biting off more than you can chew," Stark warned softly.

"Heck, you ain't much more than a nibble."

"Don't start picking your teeth yet." Stark went up on the balls of his feet, bowie extended in his right hand, his left arm out to guard. There was no way out of this now except by blood and steel.

Nickle used his left hand to flick his Stetson clear of his head. A calculated move. A hat could impede a man's vision, but it could also keep the sun from blinding him at a crucial moment. Stark left his hat in place.

Nickle's crouch was a mirror image of Stark's own. The outlaw came in grinning, weaving, waving his left hand a little as a distraction. Then his right hand started to move, darting forward in quick jabs, hooking in short tight slashes. Stark circled clear of the gully wall so he'd have plenty of room. He backpedaled, watching his opponent's footwork, the movements of his body. This was all show-off stuff, but it could still be dangerous if he wasn't careful.

Nickle stopped, still grinning, pleased with his performance. "Can't touch me, can you, Peacemaker?" he jeered.

Stark wheeled to the outside, stepped close and chopped with his blade to knock Nickle's bowie downward. He was careful to avoid the brass inlay which could trap his steel. Nickle's arm was forced toward the ground. Stark shot his left fist over it in a sharp twisting jab to Nickle's mouth. The outlaw's head rocked. He fell back a step, and a crimson trickle began at the corner of his mouth.

"First blood," Stark said.

Nickle touched his lips and stared with disbelief at the stain on his fingers. "The devil it is!" he snarled, and came in like a bucket of rattlers hurled in Stark's face, blade moving in strikes faster than the eye could follow.

No playing now, no showing off. And no more stopping at first blood, Stark sensed. Nickle was out for the kill. Nothing else would satisfy his bloodied pride.

Stark wheeled to the outside. Nickle, wise to the tactic, pivoted like he was connected to Stark, his blade driving straight in. Stark had no time for a thrust of his own. His bowie moved to intercept the flash of Nickle's blade, and steel clashed. Stark cut backhanded, but Nickle leaned his torso clear of the swipe and thrust high at Stark's throat.

Stark retreated. He didn't want to stand toe-to-toe with a foe this fast and dangerous. Nickle's rush drove him backward at almost a run, the brass-rimmed bowie seeming to come at him from all angles. He blocked and parried by reflex, arm flicking and darting to meet steel with steel. The crowd of onlookers scattered before his retreat. Dimly he heard their excited shouts and yells.

He tried to turn his knife to catch Nickle's blade in the brass inlay of his own weapon. But Nickle twisted his wrist deftly, so the flat of his bowie slid unimpeded across the rim of Stark's knife. Unexpectedly Nickle went low, lunging forward to drop to one knee, arm and body extended in a crippling slash at Stark's leg. Stark hiked his knee like he was avoiding a sweep kick in savate, then shot his leg straight out as Nickle's blade swept past beneath. The flat of his driving foot landed on face and chest, spilling Nickle over.

Stark sprang forward, knife drawn back for a killing downward thrust. Nickle's wildly slashing blade and flailing feet made him swerve clear. Before he could press in again, Nickle had scrambled to his feet. He was panting, savage, frustrated, stinging from humiliation as much as from the blows he'd taken. Maybe it would make him reckless.

Stark shifted his blade point upward, as if careless of what he was doing in the heat of action. He wanted Nickle to believe he'd unthinkingly turned his blade to where it was no longer in good position to parry or attack.

He saw Nickle's eyes narrow, then flare with triumph. Nickle came in fast, lunging hard, committing himself to a thrust he figured Stark was no longer able to parry.

Stark didn't try to parry. As Nickle's bowie streaked at him, he brought his own blade surging straight up. Its point intercepted Nickle's extended arm and transfixed his wrist from below.

Nickle let out a strangled cry of shock. Stark wrenched his blade free, hoping it was over. It wasn't. As Nickle's knife fell from his spasmed fingers, his left hand, incredibly, darted over to pluck it from the air. It came wobbling awkwardly at Stark's throat. With no recourse, Stark slashed backhanded for the neck, and Nickle reeled away and collapsed. Even when he stopped moving, his bowie was still gripped in his fist.

Stark wheeled toward the onlookers. "Any friends of his looking to settle the score?" he rasped.

There was an uneasy shifting among the outlaws. "Naw, mister," one fellow said at last. "He asked for it; you took him clean. By Godfrey, I never thought I'd see the day Blade Nickle went down under another man's knife.''

A murmur of agreement came from his companions.

''Dirk ain't going to like this,'' another hombre muttered. ''There'll be the devil to pay when he comes back.''

Stark turned toward Shed. The big man glared at him with no sign of fear, but didn't make any effort to take up where Nickle had left off.

The crowd began to disperse. A couple of the men toted Nickle's body under an overhang and left it there. Stark watched them bleakly. He had a hunch the one hombre's prophecy was going to come true; Garland wasn't going to be happy.

Had Prudence seen the fight? Stark wondered suddenly. He needed another chance to visit with her, but under Shed's vengeful eye, there was no way he could manage it for now, particularly with a guard still posted outside her prison.

Nobody had disturbed Nickle's body when Garland and Wilson returned from scouting. Fists on his hips, his gang gathered around him, the outlaw chieftain stared at the corpse for a long moment, then he came about sharply on Stark.

''What the deuce did you think you were doing?'' he stormed. ''I didn't hire you on to have you go killing off my other men.'' His yellow eyes were like flames.

Stark shrugged. ''Didn't have a choice. He called the play. Wouldn't take no for an answer.''

''The Peacemaker's right, Boss,'' one of the outlaws spoke up. ''Blade kept pushing. Stark came near showing yellow before he took him on.'' He shook his head in awe. ''Blamedest thing you ever seen!''

''I ain't interested in what kind of a dance they put on!'' Garland shouted. ''I got a dead man laying here, and nothing to show for it. That ain't the way things work in my outfit! My boys don't go killing each other off. I ought to string you up, Stark!''

Garland was on the verge of doing just what he said, Stark realized. How many of these hellions could he kill before they overwhelmed him? He tensed for one last desperate stand. He'd never be taking Prudence back to Guthrie.

"No percentage in it, Dirk," Slick Wilson advised softly. "You'd just be out another man, maybe more than that if Stark's good enough with a knife to take Blade."

Garland's head snapped toward his segundo, the blond locks of hair rippling.

Wilson didn't flinch under his glare. His lined face was unperturbed. "Could be, we'll need every gunhand we've got if things go sour," he drawled casually, with only the barest flick of his eyes toward the lean-to.

Garland's heavy shoulders heaved; his jaw muscles worked like he was chewing a piece of jerky. Then, by degrees, he relaxed. Stark sensed a lessening of the tension in the watching owlhoots. His own muscles lost some of their tautness.

"Shoot!" Garland said at last in disgusted tones. "What's everybody standing around here for? Some of you take that carcass and bury it!" He waved a thick arm at the still form under the overhang. A handful of the outlaws moved to obey his order.

As the rest of the pack dispersed, Garland stomped up to Stark. Dust clung to the sweat on his beard. He might've reined in his rage, Stark thought, but it wasn't corralled yet.

"I won't stand for no more trouble out of you, top gunhand or not!" he asserted fiercely. "Maybe I didn't lay out the rules like I should've, but that's no nevermind now. You tangle with another one of my boys, and I'll be the one to finish it. You hear what I say?"

"I hear," Stark confirmed. "Best you tell your boys the same thing. I told you, it wasn't me started this fracas."

"You let me worry about my men! You just keep your nose out of trouble from here on."

"Do my best," Stark said mildly.

Garland grunted, then turned away. "Shed!" He spotted the brawler slinking off.

Shed halted. "Yeah, Boss?"

Garland strode toward him. "Where were you when all this was going on?"

Shed's reply was inaudible as the pair of them moved away.

Stark cocked an eyebrow at Wilson. "Obliged," he offered laconically. "Why'd you take a hand?"

Wilson shifted his shoulders a bit. "What I said was true enough; we can't afford to lose good fighting men. Besides, it seemed a shame for one of our breed to go out at the end of a rope."

"You reckon there's a better way?"

"You know there is. Straight up and face-to-face against another top man with a gun."

Stark studied him shrewdly. "That's the real reason you butted in," he said softly. "You don't want me getting killed before you have a chance to find out if you can take me."

Wilson's face was still as expressionless as aged leather, but evil spirits brooded in his eyes. "They say no matter how good you are, there's always somebody faster, or a better shot. Me, I've never run into him yet."

Stark recalled the gunslick, Brazos, back in Guthrie. For a fleeting instant he felt a dark kinship with Wilson. "There's always somebody looking to make a rep for themselves by proving they're the one," he mused aloud.

"Ain't it the truth."

"But you've kept your gun holstered for the last few years," Stark went on. "You've been playing cowboy at Garland's ranch. You're getting a little long in the tooth for the gunhand's game. You're wondering if you're too old, if you've still got the skill and the reflexes to go up against a younger man, maybe even to go up against the Peacemaker."

He saw from the haunted look in Wilson's eyes that he'd hit dead center.

"I can handle any wet-behind-the-ears kid who wants to try me," Wilson said with a trace of hoarseness in his voice. "And, come right down to it, I can handle you too."

"You're forgetting we're on the same side," Stark objected mildly.

"Are we?"

Stark's nape prickled. Experienced and savvy, Wilson didn't trust him, and the aging gunhand was looking for an excuse to go up against him gun-to-gun. "You got any doubts," Stark spoke aloud, "take them up with the boss-man."

"I'll do that," Wilson promised. He pivoted away, but did it in such a fashion that he could keep Stark in the edge of his vision as he withdrew.

Stark watched him go. His neck still prickled. Wilson wouldn't need much of an excuse to come for him, and he'd earned Garland's rage by killing one of his men. His charade couldn't go on much longer. Prisoner or not, he was going to have to act and act soon while he was still alive and kicking.

Chapter Nine

Stark listened to Shed snore and knew he couldn't wait any longer. The camp was dark and silent. Jagged clouds slashed across the black sky high overhead. As on the night before, he'd bedded down away from the rest of the outlaw crew. It hadn't been hard. Following his duel with Nickle, most of the outlaws had reined clear of him. Shed, still smarting from the dressing down he must've received from Garland, had been mean and surly for the rest of the day, further discouraging any contact with his cohorts.

Stark sat up, shifting his shoulders for the benefit of any watchers as if the hard ground under his bedroll disagreed with him. He ran his eyes over the camp. He'd wanted more time to come up with a plan, but events had gotten away from him. The longer he stayed in this nest of scorpions, the more likely he was to get stung.

Shed had been a long time falling asleep, but from the sounds of his snoring, he had apparently done a good job of it at last. Stark eased erect and approached his slumbering form on cat's feet. Shed needed to be put out of action. Stark could've used his bowie on the bruiser, but killing a sleeping man—even Shed—in that fashion wasn't something he fancied having on his conscience.

He drew near Shed, and his booted foot flicked out, its power carefully calculated. Shed's whole body shuddered, and he grunted. Then his eyelids fluttered, as though the kick had only disturbed his slumber. A little bit amazed at the brute's stamina, Stark kicked again. Shed sighed and relaxed, out cold. Stark bent to pull the outlaw's gun from its holster.

"Right there, Stark," Slick Wilson's voice said softly before Stark's fingers touched the gunbutt.

Stark froze. How in thunder had the gunman crept up on him without being detected? he asked himself.

"Move away from him," Wilson ordered in the same low tones. "Did you kill him?"

"Just gave him a headache." Stark came slowly about and stepped clear of Shed's prone bulk.

Wilson stood like a specter in the gloom five yards distant. He didn't have his gun drawn, but his hands dangled loosely at his sides. The fingers of his right hand curled and uncurled rhythmically.

"Too bad I ain't heeled," Stark said quietly. "We could find out if you still have what it takes."

"Don't push your luck," Wilson advised. "I knew if you were up to something you'd have to pull it tonight. You been riding the ragged edge ever since you got here. You'd have been a fool to go on riding it any longer, and I don't figure you as a fool."

Deliberately Stark clasped his hands together in front of his belt buckle. Maybe driven by the opportunity to lord it over one of the few men he considered his peer, maybe by the same dark kinship Stark had felt earlier,

Wilson wanted to talk for the moment, rather than raise the alarm. If he could keep this confab going for a spell, Stark calculated, he might have some slim chance to turn the tables.

He didn't have any other card to play.

"What's your game?" Wilson asked probingly. His fingers still curled and uncurled as if their owner wasn't even aware of their movements.

Stark saw no reason to lie. He nodded toward the shed. "The girl."

Wilson started with surprise. "You didn't follow us; I'll lay oath to that. How'd you buy into the deal?"

"I got paid to see what you were doing hiding out up here. Just happened to be keeping an eye on things when you brought her in."

Wilson spat. "Of all the deuced luck! This was as clean of a job as I've ever seen. We get away scot-free, and then you show up."

Stark contemplated using his bowie. Tinhorn's play. He could never draw and throw before Wilson got off a shot, and Wilson wouldn't need more than one.

"It'll never work," he commented. "Garland's going to bring the lightning down on all your heads with his crazy scheme. You'll all end up hanged alongside him and his son."

"Don't count on it. He's got every angle covered."

"Except me."

Wilson gave a little jeering grin. "You're past history now, Peacemaker. Dirk won't like being fooled. I expect you'll be stretching hemp a long time before any of us. I've seen Dirk hang men before when they crossed him. It ain't pretty."

"Then you'll never know which of us is better."

Frustration twisted Wilson's features. "That bothers me. It truly does."

Casually Stark unclasped his hands and put them behind his back.

Wilson tensed. His curling fingers froze. "Get your hands back out where I can see them!" he ordered.

Stark brought his hands back around into the open and showed Wilson the .38 hideout he'd drawn from its concealed holster behind his gunbelt.

Wilson cursed, and his gunhand twitched.

"Don't try it," Stark warned. "This piece is double-action. You won't beat a dead drop."

"A hideout!" Wilson gritted. "I should've known."

"Yeah, you should've."

"Blast you, Stark!" Wilson's tone was almost pleading. "Put that up. I'll give you back your Colt. The devil with Garland. We'll settle it like it should be settled—straight up and face-to-face."

Stark shook his head in refusal. "Some other time, I might consider it. Maybe I'm wanting to know who's the better man. But you were willing to let your boss hang me just now, so I don't feel too obligated. Besides, I got Miss McKay's life to consider. Sorry, but I can't run the risk. Pull your hogleg left-handed, and drop it easy-like there in front of you."

Grudgingly Wilson started to obey. With the gun in his hand, he paused, and Stark remembered how his own reflexes had almost betrayed him when he'd been disarmed in Garland's cabin. "Don't," he advised softly.

Slowly, every muscle rigid, Wilson let the gun drop. He lifted his head to stare at Stark, and, in the gloom, his eyes seemed to blaze.

Stark knew there would be no more restraint on Wilson. A pro like Wilson, aching to prove to himself that he was still as good as his rep, couldn't take being buffaloed like this. The humiliation of it burned too deep. If he lived, he'd seek Stark out like a wolf on a scent, and the next time they met when both were packing iron,

Wilson wouldn't hesitate, no matter what the circumstances or the cost. It would be straight up and face-to-face, with only one of them walking away.

"Now turn around," Stark ordered.

Wilson didn't move.

"I won't kill you," Stark promised. "You'll wake up with a sore head, and maybe one day we can settle things between us. But not here; not now."

"We'll settle them, all right," Wilson vowed through gritted teeth. "I'll see to that." With the stiffness of a stone statue he pivoted until his back was to Stark.

The Peacemaker moved swiftly forward, palming his bowie in his left hand.

"You'll never make it out of the camp," Wilson said tightly over his shoulder.

"Almost there already," Stark answered. As Wilson, sensing his nearness, started to turn, he drove the hilt of the bowie against his temple. The gunslick collapsed limply at Stark's feet.

Stark drew a shaky breath. There were never any guarantees in trying to take a man like Wilson. He'd be dangerous until he was dead.

Stark dragged his slack form back into the shadows. Valuable minutes were escaping, but he took the time to bind and gag both his victims, using strips cut from Shed's bedding. No one else stirred in the camp. Their low voices and isolated location had kept his confrontation with Wilson from awakening any of the other outlaws. Sure of his control of the situation, Wilson hadn't bothered to alert anyone else. It was a mistake that had cost him.

Stark glanced at Garland's cabin, but there was no sign of life there. He gathered his gear. Keeping to the shadows as much as possible, he cut across the draw to Wilson's den, praying the lone guard at the lean-to wouldn't notice his skulking figure.

Under the overhang he rummaged until his hand closed gratifyingly on the familiar wooded stock of the repeating shotgun. He hefted it with satisfaction. Next to it was his revolver. He checked the loads, then slipped it thankfully into his holster, returning the hideout gun to its concealed sheath. Kneeling, he drew the bowie and rubbed its blade through the dirt to dull its sheen.

With the big knife held inconspicuously alongside his leg, he emerged from the overhang and headed toward the shed. He risked an open approach. The longer he dallied, the more likely he was to be discovered. The moon winked wanly from behind the racing clouds, which cast darting shadows across the floor of the draw. Already the night was well along. Urgency hastened his stride.

The lookout, prowling listlessly before the lean-to, straightened as he saw Stark's approaching figure.

"I'm your relief," Stark offered as he drew closer. "You can hit the sack."

The guard relaxed at his words, then tensed as he got a good look at his relief. By then it was too late for his sluggish muscles to react in time. Stark's foot moved like a striking shadow in the gloom and drove square into the owlhoot's midriff. A strangled gasp was the only sound he could muster. As he doubled forward, Stark hammered the hilt of the bowie down on his nape. Swiftly Stark bound and gagged him.

Stepping over his victim, he glided to the lean-to and rapped softly. "It's Stark!" he hissed. "Keep quiet."

He heard a flurry of movement, then the soft sounds of Prudence's breathing as he unfastened the crude lock and hauled at the door. Her thrusting palms propelled it open.

She almost sprang from her confinement, and for a fevered instant she clung to Stark tightly, as if to reassure herself of his reality. Stark had an intense, fleeting awareness of her soft form pressed against him, the silkiness of her hair just brushing his chin.

Then she drew back almost sharply. Her breath was coming rapidly, but her face was only a pale image. He saw for the first time she was handcuffed. He found the keys on the guard and released her.

"Stay with me," he whispered. "We're not out of the woods yet."

Still breathless, she nodded. "Let's get out of here!"

Stark started to reach for her hand, then thought better of taking such a liberty. He wondered if she noticed his indecision. "Come on," he told her gruffly, "we need supplies and horses."

She followed him as he moved down the draw to the rocky niche where the supplies were stored. He was gratified to note that she moved quietly. A long owlhoot had bedded down just outside the makeshift storeroom. He stirred as they approached, and Stark stepped forward and kicked out swiftly. He heard Prudence's sharply indrawn breath. The outlaw subsided without a sound. Stark fancied Prudence shied away from him as she followed him into the niche.

On his haunches, Stark fumbled in the poor light, feeling among the bags and bundles of foodstuffs. He was conscious of Prudence's nearness in the enclosed space.

"I can do this," she asserted in a whisper. "Go get the horses. I'll meet you there."

Her offer made sense, although Stark was reluctant to leave her alone.

"Go on!" she urged.

He withdrew from the rocky storehouse. Pausing by the unconscious guard, he secured the fellow's revolver and stuck it in his belt. He catfooted to the rope corral.

The horses stirred restlessly. Softly Stark clicked his tongue. In a moment the powerful figure of Red pushed past the other animals to reach him. The sorrel's quick acceptance of the nighttime visitor quieted the other horses. Stark breathed a prayer of thanks.

The saddles were carelessly stowed nearby under a tarp. Stark claimed two of them, wishing he had the time to find his own familiar hull. He saddled Red and a dun mare. The other horses grew more restless when Prudence appeared with a bulging tow sack. Stark tied it to his saddle horn. He pulled the outlaw's revolver and proffered it to Prudence. She faltered.

"Take it!" he insisted in a whisper.

She accepted the weapon and stuck it in the waistband of her jeans without comment.

From the main part of the camp, a man's voice shouted hoarsely. Another told him angrily to quit bellowing in his sleep.

Stark felt Prudence's wide eyes fasten on him. He waited for a long moment, the reins of both horses gripped in his fist. In the corral a horse gave vent to a loud neigh. Another answered it, and a ripple of motion ran through the small herd. Then, from startlingly nearby, a man's voice was raised in angry inquiry as to what was spooking the horses.

The cat was awful close to being out of the bag, Stark realized. he motioned Prudence to her horse with a sweep of his arm. She complied, clambering into the saddle with reassuring ability. He tossed her the reins, and she caught them deftly. Stark swung astride Red. He used a jabbing finger to point back down the draw, and saw Prudence nod her understanding.

"Hey, what in tarnation is going on?" The shambling figure of a man—likely the same one who had spoken moments before—emerged from the darkness. At sight of the two mounted shapes, he clawed for his gun.

Stark drew first and shot him in the chest from horseback. As the echoes resounded, and the yahoo fell, Stark wheeled Red and leaned from the saddle to slash at the rope barrier of the makeshift corral with his bowie. He switched knife for gun and blasted a shot at the racing clouds overhead. The nearest horses milled, found no way to retreat, and surged forward, breaking wide around him in a panicked rush.

Stark put Red into the stampede, pleased to see Prudence likewise racing her mare in the midst of the herd.

They tore back down the draw, away from the heart of the camp. The thundering hooves drowned any outcry from behind them, but Stark knew it would not be long in coming.

The shadowy forms of the racing horses were all about him, swerving close, baring square teeth to snap at one another in their fear and excitement. The headlong rush was dangerous in the poor light. Dust billowed up from their churning hooves.

Stark worked Red closer to Prudence's mare. Garland would have lookouts posted, and, even in the protection of the horse herd, he didn't want to ride under their guns. Besides, the momentum of the wild charge was already beginning to slow.

He spotted the black mouth of a defile emptying into the draw, and herded Prudence's mare toward it. Prudence grasped his objective and angled in that direction. Red evaded a last rear kick from a passing stallion, and they won free of the herd. Stark headed the sorrel into the gully mouth. It led steeply upward, narrowing almost immediately.

Once they were clear of the draw, Stark reined to a halt and sprang from the saddle. Tearing a branch from a stickery bush, he wiped it across the tracks they had left at the mouth of the defile. In the darkness, he knew he likely hadn't erased every trace of their passage, but he hoped it would be enough to fool a cursory searcher. Lord willing, the outlaws would think they had stayed with the stampeding herd and it would be some time before their real route was discovered. And, he hoped, no substantial efforts at pursuit could be made until the horses had been rounded up, which might not be until after daylight.

But, as soon as possible, he knew Garland and his pack, including a vengeful Wilson, would be after them. The outlaw chieftain had too much at stake to let them just ride out free and clear. Come morning, the whole bunch would be after them in full hue and cry. They were deep in Indian Territory and a long ways from anything approaching law and order, except what a man could enforce behind the barrel of a gun.

Stark stepped back into the saddle, sparing a moment to replace the two shells he'd fired in their escape. He'd dropped one owlhoot for sure in the brief bit of gunplay, but that still left well nigh onto a score of gun-hungry killers to contend with.

Shrouded in darkness, Stark led Prudence up out of the defile and into the surrounding woods.

Chapter Ten

" " I haven't thanked you,'' Prudence said tightly as they skirted a tree-strewn bluff on the outskirts of the hill country. The morning sun, shining down through the branches, cast auburn highlights from her dark hair.

Despite her ordeal, she looked quite fetching on her mare, Stark mused, and would've looked even more so if it weren't for the stiff disapproval evident in the rigid lines of her trim figure.

"You can deduct your gratitude from that bill you're going to send me,'' Stark said sourly in answer to her.

She flinched, then looked at him squarely. "How many of those men did you kill?'' Her tone bore only the slightest hint of accusation.

Stark blinked. "I figure I did for the one I shot. The other three I put out of action are most likely back on their feet and out there behind us, on our trail with the rest of the gang.'' He eyed her from the edge of his vision.

She relaxed as if in relief. "I . . . I was afraid you had killed that man you kicked while he was asleep."

"Would've been one less to be after us," Stark pointed out. "But I'm not as bloodthirsty as you seem to think."

She had the grace to color a little. "I should've known that," she admitted softly. "I did see you disarm that man in Guthrie. I suppose it would've been almost as easy for you to kill him."

"Easier," Stark growled.

"Well, I am grateful for all you've done. I'm sorry if I offended you. I certainly shouldn't have much sympathy for those men." She broke off with a shudder that was the first human reaction he had seen from her since that brief moment when she had clung tightly to him upon being released.

"I suppose my sympathy should be for poor Temple Houston," she went on.

"Houston?" Stark said more sharply than he'd intended. "What's he got to do anything?"

"He attempted to rescue me when I was abducted."

Stark listened as she described the harrowing events of that evening in Guthrie, "So, Houston threw down on them, did he?" Stark commented musingly when she finished.

"Yes, he was very brave." Her face clouded. "I hope he's all right."

"He's always impressed me as being hardheaded. Likely, it'll take more than being sandbagged in an alley to put him out of business."

She frowned at his tone and didn't reply.

Stark twisted about in his saddle to check their back-trail. He had kept them moving steadily during the hours of darkness, wending their way through the hills. So far, there had been no sign of pursuit. He didn't let that fool him. As they neared the edge of the rough terrain, he had slowed their pace to let the horses rest.

Their riders needed a rest too, he reflected sourly. He could feel it in the soreness of his bones and joints, and in the grainy roughness of his eyes. And, though she hadn't complained, he could see it in the haggard cast of Prudence's pretty face and the tired slump of her slender shoulders.

But they couldn't afford much rest anytime soon.

Stark pulled up as they emerged from the mouth of a tree-lined draw. Ahead was open country—the rolling prairie that stretched off into the haze of the morning. They'd be mighty exposed out there on the grasslands.

"Can't we stay in the hills?" Prudence might've read his misgivings.

"We'd just be playing cat and mouse with them. The cat usually wins. "We've got to try to get out of Indian Territory; reach some place where there's some law to back us up."

"Is there any place like that nearby?"

Stark shook his head grimly. There were communities, right enough, in the Indian Lands, but most of them didn't have more than a part-time sheriff or constable to enforce the law. Garland and his desperadoes would eat a lawman like that for breakfast. Nor would Andrew Blaine's cowhands stand a chance, even if he and Prudence could reach the ranch headquarters.

"Best thing we can do is head for Guthrie," he advised aloud. "Garland's got a small army. It'll take a passel of Nix's deputies to make them think twice about lassoing you a second time."

She squared her shoulders resolutely. "Very well."

Stark figured again she made a fine picture sitting there on her mare. He shook the thought aside. He couldn't afford to be distracted by the beauty of his charge.

She turned and looked at him sharply, catching him in his reverie. "What's wrong?"

"Look," he said flatly, "there's liable to be more killing before this is done. You need to get used to the idea. We might not be able to avoid it."

Her prim chin lifted. "I'm quite aware we might have to fight. But there's a difference between defending yourself and killing a sleeping man who can't do you any harm at the moment."

Stark put aside a surge of irritation. What she said was true. Why did it irk him so much to have her say it?

He heeled Red forward out onto the grasslands. Prudence brought the mare beside him. The horses were holding up well, but they'd need to graze before the day was out. Stark wished he'd been able to procure a couple more of the outlaw horses so they could switch off on them and give Red and the mare a chance to rest while they traveled.

Under the circumstances, Prudence had done a fine job of stocking their larder, and they were in pretty good shape for supplies. Of course, if Garland and his crew caught up with them, they'd never have time to fret about starving to death, Stark reminded himself bleakly. He wondered if it was the presence of the woman that had put him in such a dark mood.

He set the horses at an easy lope, wanting to get some miles between them and the hills as soon as possible. A watcher on the slopes would be able to spot them for quite a distance. He would've liked to push their mounts even faster, but they might need to have some energy in reserve later on.

Where the rolling terrain allowed, he kept ridges and hogbacks between them and their backtrail. When the hills were far behind them, he slowed their pace. The night's clouds had vanished as though they'd never been, leaving a stark blue expanse with no relief from the glaring sun, which seemed to grow hotter and larger as it slid slowly across the sky. Perspiration gleamed on the soft curve of Prudence's cheek. She didn't have a hat to shield her face from the sun's glare. After a time she managed to secure her dark hair atop her head. Stark found his eyes drawn to the sweeping lines of her smooth neck. It was already growing red.

"You'll burn," he told her impulsively, undoing his kerchief and offering it to her. "Here, tie this around your neck."

She appeared flustered at his attention. With a quick smile she took the kerchief and did as he suggested. Stark looked away. He fancied the sun had grown suddenly hotter.

"I wish there was some way to get word to my father," she spoke up unexpectedly.

"We'll take care of that as soon as we can. First order of business is to get you someplace safe. We're a long way from accomplishing that just yet."

"I know," she conceded, then glanced over at him. "How did you ever come to be in Garland's camp? I don't understand anything except that you pretended to join them."

Briefly Stark recounted being hired by Andrew Baine and the ranchers he represented. Her head cocked, she listened attentively.

"Was that Mr. Blaine you were dining with in Guthrie?"

"Yeah, that was him."

She gave him a brief look, trying to read him in some fashion. "Temple—I mean, Mr Houston—was very impressed with the way you disarmed that gunman. He said you used something called savate."

Stark nodded, wondering at her interest. "When I was a kid, working the cattle ranches up in Montana, I win-

tered with an old Frenchman. We were snowed in at a
line shack lots of the time, with not much to do. I'd seen
him whip a bigger man using just his feet, and I asked
him to show me how. He taught me a lot about the art
of savate. Then, later, I went to Paris and studied under
a gentleman named Joseph Charlemont. He's one of the
best in the world. The Pinkertons sent me over there to
work under him so I could train some of their other
operatives in his techniques.'' Stark shifted uncomfort-
ably in his saddle. ''Have you ever seen Paris?''

She blinked with apparent surprise. ''Oh, yes. My father and I traveled abroad the summer before I started
my studies in law.''

Stark regarded her curiously. ''Did your father want
you to be a lawyer?''

''He wanted me to have training in one of the profes-
sions. He was certain that one day women would have
to make their way in the business world just like men.''

Privately Stark hoped not. ''And you chose the legal
profession?'' he queried aloud.

' 'Well, Father chose it for me, but I really didn't
mind. I admire him a great deal, and the idea of studying
law appealed to me.''

Stark recalled his earlier reflection on the problems a
young attractive woman would face in the male environment of legal education. ''Law school must've been difficult.''

Her face went stern, like it had when she'd confronted
U.S. Prosecutor Damon Rasters on Stark's behalf. ''The
studies were difficult enough,'' she said. ''What made it
worse was the attitude of most of the other students who
refused to admit that a woaman could do just as well as
any of them.'' Her features and voice tightened under
the strain of her recollections. ''I had to work twice as
hard as any of them to pass every course—first, to prove
that I could do the work, and second, to prove that being

female didn't have to make any difference in such matters.''

''If I was a betting man, I'd wager you graduated near
the top of your class,'' Stark said seriously.

Her head came quickly about. ''The very top,'' she
asserted with unapologetic pride. Her eyes seemed to
challenge him to comment.

''Why did you come to Oklahoma?'' Stark asked
mildly.

She considered the question. ''I wanted to prove I
could make it on my own after getting out of law school.
I didn't want to have to rely on my father to give me a
job. That would've made all of my efforts at school seem
wasted. Most of the established firms in Kansas didn't
care to have a woman associated with them, particularly
one who might know more about the law than the senior
partners did. I heard there was a need for lawyers
in Oklahoma Territory, and I reasoned that if I succeeded
here, it wouldn't be because of any nepotism. My father
was against my coming at first, but I just had to do
it.'' She broke off and bit her lip. ''Now I wonder if I
did the right thing. If I hadn't come here, none of this
would've happened.''

Stark was a little surprised at her faltering tone. ''Garland would've come after you no matter where you
were,'' he pointed out.

''I suppose you're right,'' she murmured thoughtfully,
and made a visible effort to put her troubling doubts
aside. ''What about you?'' she inquired. ''Often, as now,
you sound like an educated man. You don't always talk
like a—''

''Hired gun?'' Stark cut in dryly.

''Perhaps,'' she said in arch tones, and widened her
eyes expectantly for a response.

Stark shrugged. ''Sometimes I'm hired by wealthy
and educated individuals. It pays to be able to consort

with them on their terms. I've knocked around and picked up the basics of a sound education over the years, I suppose. And I studied law and other subjects when I was with the Pinkertons.''

Ahead of them he spotted a scraggly line of cotton-woods and underbrush that marked the meandering course of a creek. He pointed with his chin. ''We'll stop up there for a spell to water the horses.''

''That sounds wonderful.'' She glanced apprehensively back over her shoulder. ''Is there any chance we've lost them, or that they won't be able to pick up our trail?''

Stark moved his head back and forth. ''Garland's bound to have some good trackers in that bunch. It might take them some time, but they'll find our trail,'' he predicted grimly.

The narrow creek had cut a twelve-foot bed through the red soil of the prairie. Leaning cottonwoods extended their branches out over the rapidly flowing water. Stark spotted a break in the brush and put Red down the steep bank. Dismounting, he loosened the cinch and let the sorrel drink, noting with approval that Prudence handled her mare the same way.

Stark dropped to one knee and drank some himself, cupping the cool water to his lips like one of Gideon's soldiers, right hand resting on the butt of his Colt. He splashed more water onto his face, using the palm of his hand to scrub away some of the dust and grit that had accumulated over the hours and miles.

Prudence wet the kerchief he'd given her and wiped her face. She dunked the kerchief, wrung it out, then pressed it against the back of her sun-reddened neck. She closed her eyes and sighed with thankfulness. ''That feels heavenly.''

Stark swallowed hard at the image of her shapely figure in the revealing men's shirt and jeans. "I'll take the horses up and let them graze," he said.

Atop the far bank he hobbled both animals and left them contentedly chomping at the thick buffalo grass. He tarried a few moments longer, scanning the surrounding countryside, before descending once more to the stream.

"Hungry?" Prudence asked from where she knelt over the tow sack of supplies. She had done something to freshen herself, and she looked bright and pretty and very fetching there in the shade by the sun-dappled water.

"Famished," Stark answered her. He realized it was near noon. Outside of munching on some cold biscuits as they negotiated the hills early that morning, they had eaten nothing. "Go easy," he added. "We don't know how long we'll have to make our supplies last. I don't want to risk shooting any game until there's no other choice."

Within a matter of minutes she had laid out a conservative repast of salted of ham and a can of peaches. Seated by the creek, they shared the fruit for dessert.

Prudence popped the final slice of fruit in her mouth, licked her fingers delicately, then reached over to trail them in the water to cleanse the last bit of syrup from them. Looking up, she caught Stark watching her and gave a hesitant, almost shy smile.

"Not quite as fancy as the restaurant in Guthrie," Stark quipped.

"You can make amends once we're back there," she teased in turn, then suddenly blushed and looked away.

"We better get moving." Stark rose abruptly. "Bury the can, and I'll unhobble the horses."

It would be pleasant to forget the pack of outlaws somewhere on their backtrail, he reflected as they left the creek behind. How long had it been since he'd enjoyed the breeze and the sunshine, and the company of a pretty girl?

"Oh, look! Prudence exclaimed. "There are riders!"

Stark followed her pointing finger, then unshipped his field glasses and raised them to his eyes. Three horsemen were moving along the crest of distant ridge. It took Stark a moment to get them spotted in the glasses, then focus in on them. The trio looked to be cowpunchers headed back the way he and the girl had come. Likely they worked for one of the ranches leasing land from the tribes.

"Can we ask them for help?" Prudence queried once he had reported his observations to her.

Stark calculated speed and distance. Having three more guns siding them was an appealing notion, although the odds still wouldn't mean much to Garland if he caught up with them. And to intercept the cowboys would take time—as well as effort from their horses— that they couldn't afford to spare, particularly since they'd be riding back toward their pursuers if they went after the punchers.

"Too far off," he decided reluctantly.

"We could catch them!" Prudence objected immediately. "And they'd certainly assist us, or maybe take us to some sanctuary!"

Stark set his jaw. "Overhauling them would only give Garland more time to catch up with us. And even the five of us wouldn't stand a chance against his gang. We'd likely just be signing those poor fellows' death warrants, not to mention our own."

"But—"

"We don't have time to argue!" Stark cut her off curtly.

"Excuse me, Mr. Stark!" she snapped.

Stark ignored her and put his boots to Red. When she

drew her mare up alongside the sorrel some hundred yards farther on, her face was set and tight, her carriage rigid. Stark scowled in exasperation at her muleheadedness. The breeze had turned hot and unpleasant.

Chapter Eleven

With occasional stops to rest the horses, they pushed on over the prairie as the sun continued its slide across the sky and finally sank from sight. In its wake it left an artist's sweep of building clouds backlit by pink fading to blue, and then purple.

"Is it safe to stop for dinner?" Prudence asked as twilight crept in slowly to cover the plains.

Stark nodded. "We'll eat a bite, then push on for a spell."

"At night?" she questioned.

"I'm hoping we can gain some on them," he explained. "They may not be able to track us at night, particularly if we slant off the route we've been following."

"We've come a long way," she pointed out. "Are you sure they're back there?"

"I'm sure."

Dinner was coffee, beans, and reheated biscuits. She

prepared the meal over a tiny fire in the shelter of a ridge while he saw to the horses. The mare was holding up well, he noted with satisfaction. Providence had smiled on him when he'd chosen her from the outlaw herd. As yet, he had no real concerns over Red's condition; the big sorrel had stood him in good stead over a lot of miles through the years.

He extinguished the fire as soon as the cooking was done, and allowed an hour's rest while darkness claimed the sky, and the stars gradually appeared as thousands of pinpricks of light.

"Let's head out," he ordered at last. "We'll travel till midnight, then make camp."

For once she didn't question his decision. He let the horses walk as they moved out. The prairie was a pale ghostly expanse, bordered by gloom. Grass waved eerily in the night breeze, and almost-seen shapes seemed to lurk just beyond the range of vision. Once Stark glimpsed a distant fire but made no move to investigate. Strangers out here were just as likely to be hostile as otherwise, and even law-abiding folks would be ready to sling lead at newcomers riding up on their camp in the night.

He could tell by the looseness of Prudence's silhouetted figure when she began to doze in the saddle. The moon was high overhead, and his own eyelids were heavy. Close to twenty-four hours they had been on the move now, he estimated.

When he tugged Red to an easy halt, Prudence's mare stopped as well, its head hanging a little. Prudence swayed in the saddle but didn't awaken. Stark slipped to the ground and rounded the sorrel to get to her. He reached up with the intent of shaking her gently, but at his touch, she went limp, sagging down off the mare into his arms.

Stark cradled her. She felt surprisingly light and fragile. Gently he lowered her to the grass, hoping she wouldn't rouse at that awkward moment. But she only stirred slightly and made a soft sound of contentment. Stark tugged her bedroll free and spread the blanket. He placed her on it and folded it over her. He used a saddlebag as a makeshift pillow. The thick grass was soft enough to make a good mattress. She did little more than sigh as he got her settled. Exhaustion had claimed her.

At their campsite, Stark had chosen a secluded hollow buried in a series of rolling grassy ridges. He unsaddled the horses and hobbled them. Having been watered once at the stream, and later at a convenient buffalo wallow, they would be all right until morning. He himself stretched out with his shotgun at his side. Red made a pretty fair watchdog, and Stark knew he needed to get some sleep himself. His last waking thought was of how soft and defenseless Prudence had felt in his arms.

He awoke to find the pale light of early morning claiming the hollow. He became aware that Prudence was sitting up, her blanket over her knees, which were pulled to her chest. She was regarding him with puzzled, sleepy eyes. Her dark hair was touseled.

"How did I get here?" she asked in bewilderment. "The last thing I remember is riding in the darkness. It seemed like we'd been going forever . . ."

"We camped about midnight." Stark enjoyed the image of her drowsy beauty.

She lifted a corner of the blanket. "You . . . did this?"

"Couldn't see any point in waking you up just so you could go to bed."

She looked away in apparent embarrassment. "I'm sorry I put you to so much trouble," she murmured. "I'll try to do better."

"You did fine," Stark assured her. "I was about ready to fall off my horse myself."

The last was a lie, but the compliment had been genuine. For a lady lawyer she was doing right well under the circumstances.

She put the blanket aside and stretched luxuriously. Stark turned his eyes away and got to his feet.

"Breakfast?" she asked, pushing her fingers through her hair.

"Just a quick one," Stark consented. 'I'm going up the ridge and have a look-see behind us."

Their backtrail was clear so far as he could make out through the field glasses. He felt a bit relieved, but they were still under way by the time the first yellow sunbeams were slanting across the prairie.

Prudence appeared much recovered after the half-night's sleep they had enjoyed. At one point she tugged at the revolver she still carried tucked in her waistband. "Do I have to carry this any longer? It's uncomfortable."

"Keep it close to you, no matter what, until we're safe."

"Are you sure we're not safe yet?"

"Pretty sure," Stark said in a tone that didn't brook discussion. He cast his eyes at a towering butte looming ahead of them. "I'll check again from up yonder." He pointed at its summit.

He reined in when they reached the base of the formation. It covered several acres and reached a height of nearly fifty feet.

"You can rest here while I look," he suggested.

Prudence shook her head. "No, I'll go with you."

Stark shrugged and urged Red up the steep trail that buffalo and livestock had worn over the centuries. She maneuvered the mare behind him until he halted just below the summit.

"Why are we stopping?"

"Don't want to skyline ourselves. Somebody might be looking through field glasses of their own."

In a low crouch, shotgun in hand, he made his way across the rough tabletop of the butte. Throwing a look back, he saw that she was still with him and doing an admirable job of staying low.

In the shelter of a sandstone boulder, he unlimbered the field glasses and made a slow sweep of the country they had traveled. Abruptly he jerked the glasses back to focus on the spot he had just covered.

"Blast!"

Briefly her hand touched his shoulder then quickly withdrew. "What is it?"

"Some yahoo with two horses, coming in on our tail like a hound dog on a scent," he answered bitterly.

Through the glasses he could make out the tiny figure, mounted on one horse and leading the other at a gallop. How this hombre had managed to stay on their trail during the nighttime hours didn't matter. Plainly he had used two horses to close the gap between them, switching from one to the other to let each rest in turn. Both he and the animals must be run almost ragged, but Stark didn't doubt that he'd have the strength to pull a trigger once he got his prey within his sights. And that time might not be long in coming. He was almost within long rifle range now.

Silently Stark berated himself for letting one of the enemy get so close. The hombre was making a beeline for the butte, and Stark could imagine him gazing up at its crest and wondering if his quarry had gone to ground there.

Stark waited a few moments to be sure. He was conscious of Prudence's tense presence close beside him. At last their pursuer's features swam clearly into view. Stark recognized the whiskered mulish face of one of Garland's pack. He didn't know the owlhoot's name, but that didn't matter either.

He set the binoculars aside and picked up the shotgun,

levering it so a solid load would be under the hammer. Blinking to refocus his vision, he settled the brass-shod butt against his shoulder. Allowing for the downhill shot, and the speed of his target, he set his sights.

"Wait!" Prudence exclaimed as the full import of what he planned sank home. "You can't—"

"This one ain't sleeping," Stark said with a growl, and pulled the trigger.

The shotgun roared. Below, the tiny figure of the horseman flew backward off his horse as though he'd been yanked by a cowboy's lariat. Both horses kept running, veering apart in opposite directions.

With a sickness in his gut, Stark lowered the shotgun and turned to Prudence. Her expression was stricken. "Look," he said coldly. "That fellow would've killed me the first chance he got. Then he'd take you back to Garland. I didn't see any point in giving him that chance!"

She stared at him as if he'd grown horns.

Hang it, he thought. Killing from a distance didn't set well with him either. Couldn't she see that? And why should what she thought matter to him in the first place?

He snapped the glasses back to his eyes. The horses had stopped running, but they were far enough away to dash any hopes he had of rounding them up to add to their tiny remuda. He focused the binoculars at a greater distance and felt his muscles go taut. Another rider with a spare mount was headed unerringly toward them. And far behind him was just the sort of cloud of dust a bunch of riders could raise even on the grassy plains.

The lone horseman wasn't within rifle range yet, but he would be before long. And Garland and the rest of his men must be eating up the miles farther back.

Tersely Stark explained this to Prudence as they hurried to their horses. She listened readily enough, but her face was pale, and she didn't speak. Stark had no time to try to read her.

He sent Red recklessly down the trail off the butte, leaning back in the saddle so the sorrel wouldn't over-balance. Prudence's mare reached the bottom only yards behind Red in a miniature landslide of dirt and rocks.

In the distance Stark could make out what looked to be some sort of broken terrain. He led the way toward it at a gallop. If his calculations were right, they should be able to reach it ahead of Garland's pack. Once there they could try to shake their pursuers. Although, he mused sourly, so far he hadn't had much success at achieving that goal. Garland must have some top-notch trackers riding for him. Likely, the man he'd shot and the other rider were a couple of his best.

The thick buffalo grass fell away beneath Red's pounding hooves. Prudence rode alongside him. Stark cast frequent looks back over his shoulder, but saw noth-ing. He hoped he had succeeded in placing the butte between them and their pursuers. The body of the outlaw he'd shot from the saddle would betray their presence, however, and no doubt lead the second horseman to re-double his efforts to close in.

Beside him, Prudence's mare missed her stride and faltered awkwardly. Stark realized the animal was going down. He reined Red hard over, reaching out with one long arm. He glimpsed Prudence's startled face and saw her sudden understanding of what he was attempting. She leaned far toward him, and his arm encircled her slender waist. He felt her weight pull against his shoul-der. He swept her clear of the saddle just as the mare hit the ground in a somersaulting roll of flailing hooves and waving tail.

Remotely Stark caught the sound of the distant report. It confirmed what he already knew. He could feel Pru-dence's yielding form pressed against his side.

"Hang on!" he shouted. "Your horse was shot!"

Surprise showed on Prudence's face even as she reached to grasp at handholds on the saddle.

"Get on behind me!" Stark ordered.

After a scramble, and a twisting heave of his arm and shoulder, she managed to straddle the saddle behind Stark. She wrapped her arms around his middle and clung tightly as he heeled the big sorrel into a dead run.

Stark felt a numbing sense of defeat. That second horseman, probably from atop the butte, had shot Prudence's mare. He'd used a Sharps or some other kind of buffalo gun, Stark figured. The range was too great for most repeaters, and had been awful long for even a buffalo gun. Doubtless the rifleman had hoped to leave Prudence afoot, and then drill Stark as he turned back to rescue her. It had been a pro's move, and it might yet pay off.

"Stay low!" Stark bent over the saddle horn and felt Prudence flatten herself against his back. Her hair brushed his cheek.

Something went past them in the air like an outsized wasp. The muted sound of the shot came rumbling on its heels. The sharpshooter had tried for Red. But the heavy slug had lost much of its power. They were pulling beyond the range of even the big buffalo gun.

Another shot followed with a rapidity that showed the shooter knew how to reload with an expert's speed. But there was only the sound of the shot. Stark thought the bullet must've fallen short.

He let Red slow a fraction. They were out of range, but they were reduced to one horse. Their chances of outrunning Garland and his hounds had all but vanished.

Prudence drew back from him a bit stiffly. He straightened in the saddle. "You all right?" he asked over his shoulder.

He sensed her nod; then came her breathless voice:

"Yes." She hesitated. "That was what the first man would've tried if he'd gotten near enough, isn't it?"

"Yep, that or something mighty close.

"My poor mare," she said after a moment, then asked, "What can we do?"

"Try to reach that rough terrain up ahead," Stark told her. He didn't have an answer as to what they'd do then.

She remained silent, as though becoming aware of the full import of their predicament. Then her arms tightened determinedly around him, urging him on.

He kept Red to a grueling pace, although the big sorrel, already weary, was beginning to labor under the double load. Behind them the sharpshooter would be descending from the butte to take up the pursuit on his two horses. If he got within rifle range before they reached cover, then the chase would be over.

The broken ground drew nearer. It appeared to be a rugged stretch of brush-choked draws and gullies backed by steep forested hills. Dark, ugly outcroppings of boulders scarred the faces of the slopes.

Foam flecked Red's jaws, and Stark could feel a rare tremor in the stallion's muscles. With a final burst of power Red cleared a deep narrow gully that served as a natural boundary for the broken lands.

Stark pulled the panting stallion to a halt. He dismounted and murmured his thanks to the winded sorrel. As Prudence clambered out of the saddle, Stark pulled his shotgun from its scabbard and turned to stare back across the grasslands. The muscles of his face felt hard and tight. The familiar cold determination to survive was welling up in him.

Prudence started to speak. She broke off as she saw the cast of his features.

They'd run as far as they could for now, Stark thought grimly. It was time for him to see if he could dampen their enemies' enthusiasm a bit.

Chapter Twelve

Temple Houston rode into the trouble town of Corner and gazed about with distaste. Late-afternoon shadows were stretching across the landscape, and they seemed only to emphasize the squalor and decadence of the place.

Two disreputable-looking men were conferring on some no doubt illicit topic in front of the saloon. They broke off their conversation to study him. He saw their eyes fall to the twin Colts he had donned to ride the trail. They edged away as he watched them steadily. Likely they took him for some well-armed gambler, or a fancy shootist, or a lawman. He didn't care which.

He dismounted from his Appaloosa, keeping an eye on the pair. They disappeared from sight around the corner of the saloon. They'd probably be making tracks over the border into Indian Territory within a handful of minutes, he mused sourly.

He put the heels of his palms against his back and stretched, arching his spine. The hours in the saddle had stiffened him. It had been too long since his younger days in Texas when he'd served as Brazoria County Attorney and often helped hunt down the very lawbreakers he prosecuted. Too much time playing big-city lawyer, he told himself.

He shed his duster and undid his long-tailed coat from behind his saddle. Shrugging into it, he studied the saloon. Rumor and hunch and a few hard facts had brought him here; those and a steely resolve to rescue Prudence McKay and get retribution for the contemptuous treatment he had received at the hands of the burly miscreant who had struck him down.

The ease with which he had been overpowered still rankled. To it had been added a frustration that grew steadily as he exhausted all means within the law of apprehending Prudence's abductors. Evett Nix had sent out posses and assigned a good number of his deputies to the case, but they had come up empty-handed. There was no trail to follow, the tracks having been lost in the tangle of prints and ruts left by the heavy traffic coming in and out of Guthrie. Nor had any solid leads developed.

Houston himself was one of the few witnesses, and to his chagrin he had been able to do little beyond describing the mysterious masked figures. He knew one of them was big and packed the punch of a prizefighter; other than that, he had been unable to supply any identifying characteristics. Other witnesses had seen a large group of horsemen leaving town, but nothing had come of this information. Prudence and her captors seemed to have vanished off the face of the earth.

Logic told Houston that the only place where a gang such as this one could effectively disappear was west of Hell's Fringe in Indian Territory. His career as a lawyer had brought him into contact with no small number of lowlifes and criminal sorts who lurked on the edges, or all the way outside, of the law. He had sought out these contacts and used whatever form of persuasion best suited the circumstances to glean information about the mysterious band of raiders.

He had picked up vague rumors of a big outlaw gang hidden out in the remote vastness of the Lands. They weren't much to go on, but he had nothing else. Closing his law office until further notice, he'd set out, traveling by train and finally by horseback to reach this shabby backwater of purgatory.

Corner was a crossroads of sorts, where he hoped to pick up more than the whispered rumors that had brought him this far.

Gazing at the saloon, he ran his hand under his hair and across the back of his neck, feeling the sweat and grime that had layered there. The image of Prudence as he'd last seen her—struggling helplessly in the grips of her captors—flashed into his mind.

He had spotted her leaving her office that evening and had hurried to catch up, hoping to persuade her to accept another offer of dinner. Her beauty attracted him, and her keen mind intrigued him. They were a rare combination. Her legal education, which matched his own, was also something unusual to find in a woman. Having seen her at work in the courtroom, he knew her to be a barrister of no small skill. He had never crossed blades with her in that arena, but he felt she would be a worthy opponent.

As a dinner companion she had been charming and gracious, although the occasion had been partially spoiled by James Stark's clash with the swaggering gunman. Could Prudence see anything in a mercenary such as Stark? he found himself wondering.

Shaking the thought aside, he strode into the saloon. For a moment he stood getting his bearings. It had been a good spell since he'd frequented a dive of this sort. Few of the patrons cared to meet his gaze. A cheap floozy started toward him, but he sent her away with a shake of his head.

"Whiskey," he told the mean-looking bald bartender.

The fellow served him a shot of cheap rotgut, probably brewed out back in the jungle of cottonwoods, Houston guessed. He downed it without flinching.

"Another."

"Just passing through?" the barkeep asked agreeably as he complied.

"Ain't we all?" Houston said with a grin.

"Yeah, I reckon," the fellow agreed wryly.

Houston continued to josh him, using his natural ability of conversing with any man at his own level, from president to owlhoot, when it suited his purposes to do so.

"Who's got the most men riding under him in these parts?" he inquired finally.

The barkeep frowned as he considered the question. "Take your pick," he suggested with a shrug. "Lots of outfits operating in these parts, some larger than others."

"I'm looking for a big group—a dozen men at least."

"Don't know what to tell you." The fellow paused thoughtfully. "But you ain't the first been asking questions along those lines. The Peacemaker himself was standing right where you are not too many days ago."

"Stark?" Houston said in surprise. "What'd he want here?"

A furtive look crossed over the bartender's battered face, as if he was having second thoughts about speaking so openly to a stranger. But he still went ahead and answered. "Said something about some old-time Kansas badmen, is all I recollect."

"Who was that?" Houston demanded as if he was questioning a hostile witness in a trial. He wanted one more answer before this source dried up like a seep in the summer.

"Dirk Garland," the barkeep said automatically. Then he scowled dangerously. "That's all I know, mister." He wheeled away.

Houston didn't press the issue. To do so would've invited trouble, and there was no benefit that could come from tangling with the hardcase barman. He turned his back to the bar, sipping his drink. He wondered what Stark was doing looking for some over-the-hill outlaw leader.

A wiry cowpuncher left his cronies at a poker table and sauntered toward the door. As he passed Houston, his eyes met those of the lawyer, and he gave a barely discernable jerk of his head toward the door. Houston kept his face impassive and watched him leave. The cowboy didn't look back.

Houston finished his drink, dropped coins on the bar, and moved toward the door. No one appeared to be paying undue attention to him. He stepped into the hot outside air, eyes flicking about him, right hand resting on the pearl handle of one of his Colts.

The cowpuncher was nowhere to be seen. Houston scowled, questioning silently if he'd misread the fellow's surreptitious signal. Casually he paced along the front of the building. As he reached the corner there was a soft whistle from alongside the structure. The cowpoke was leaning against the wall, waiting for him. He jerked his head to motion Houston forward.

Stepping carefully amid the trash that littered the alley, Houston went to meet him. The narrow passage smelled of waste and decay. He narrowed his eyes inquiringly as he drew near the cowpoke.

"You're Temple Houston, ain't you?" the fellow said in low tones.

Houston gave a clipped nod.

"Yep, I knew I recognized you," the cowboy said with satisfaction. "I was in the Cabinet Saloon in Woodward when you and Jack Love shot it out with the Jennings Brothers. That was sure some dustup, Mr. Houston! Never seen nothing like it—you standing there, big as life, not ducking or dodging, just pumping lead at them polecats!''

Houston nodded in acknowledgment. A number of people had witnessed that altercation. Amazingly, no bystanders had been hit by stray bullets. Both Jennings Brothers had gone down.

''I overheard you and the barkeep in there,'' his admirer went on. ''Don't rightly know what your game is, but I didn't figure it'd be good to go talking in front of everyone. I might be able to tell you something you'd be interested in hearing.''

''What's that?''

''I go by Hap. I work one of the ranches in the Lands. Few days ago, when I was on the back part of the spread, I done seen a big bunch of horsemen heading north, deeper into the Lands.''

''How many?'' Houston asked tightly, scenting a trail at last.

Hap shrugged his bony shoulders. ''Twelve, maybe fifteen. Funny thing was, they had a woman with them.''

Houston resisted the impulsive urge to grab and shake him. ''Was she all right?'' he demanded.

''She was alive, was about all I could see.''

''Dark brown hair?''

''Yeah, that's right. I spotted them from a-ways off and did my best to ride clear of them. They were a rough crew if I ever saw one. Leader was a big man with long yellow hair. Don't know if they saw me or not.''

''Where were you?''

Houston listened as Hap described the approximate location. He still had some more riding in front of him, he realized. He'd be heading deep into the lawless Lands.

"What about it, Mr. Houston?" said Hap. "They the ones you looking for?"

"Yeah," Houston told him. "They are."

Where was the sharpshooter? Stark questioned to himself. He tried to still the prickle of unease that lifted the hairs on his neck.

"What's wrong?" Prudence's soft voice whispered from behind him where he crouched.

Stark left off scanning the prairie; it wasn't going to do any good now. He glanced back at Prudence. "Too much time has passed. He's not coming in like I expected."

"What happened to him?" Her eyes were wide with concern.

Good question, Stark mused. He had selected a rocky niche in the broken terrain that gave them a commanding view of the grasslands they had just crossed. The shadows of late afternoon cloaked the hills at their backs. He had planned to ambush the sharpshooter when he appeared on their backtrail. With the outlaw's two horses in addition to Red, they would have a good chance of outdistancing Garland and the rest of his crew. He had lain in wait, shotgun at ready, scanning the prairie ceaselessly.

He had seen nothing. The sharpshooter should've showed himself long before now. He seemed to have vanished like some pagan wind spirit.

"Did he turn back?" Prudence persisted.

Stark shook his head. "Likely he figured out I'd be waiting for him, and swung wide so as to keep us from seeing him." Stark waved a hand to indicate the acres of rough land about them. "There's a good chance he's out there somewhere looking to draw a bead on us."

"Then . . . we need to keep going?"

"Nope." Stark was firm. "Can't afford to have him

this close on our tails. I've got to try to flush him out so I can take care of him.''

Prudence didn't argue the need for further violence. She gave a nod of bleak acceptance.

Stark looked toward the west where the sun hung low in the sky. He spoke his thoughts aloud since he knew Prudence would question him if he didn't. ''I don't have time to play games with him. Garland and the rest of his men will be catching up before too long. I have to get him to show himself.''

He studied the terrain, then lifted his eyes to the rugged wooded hills, trying to put himself in the cunning mind of the sharpshooter. In his foe's place, he would've sought the high ground to spot his prey. He'd lay odds that the outlaw was lurking somewhere on one of the hillsides. There were a good dozen sites of concealment Stark could pick out. The sniper might be in any one of them.

Stark drew a deep breath. ''Watch the slopes,'' he told Prudence. ''I'm going to give him a target.''

Before she could object, or his nerve could fail him, he clambered atop the large boulder that sheltered them. He crouched there in the open, feeling naked and exposed, trying to act as if he were looking for a safe route over the rough ground.

How long would it take the rifleman to see him and swing the buffalo gun to bear? He gave it a slow count of four, then dropped flat and rolled off the boulder in a single burst of movement.

With a banshee scream a ricochet gouged a foot-long scar across the stone where he'd just crouched.

''There!'' Prudence cried, and pointed.

Stark had already spotted the telltale cloud of powdersmoke billowing up from an outcropping of boulders on the nearest hill. He swallowed hard. The sharpshooter had been fast and accurate. Another heartbeat of time on the boulder, and he would've gone down like Prudence's mare.

Stark jerked the shotgun to his shoulder, levered, and fired. He rode the recoil and worked the lever and trigger again, sending a spray of buckshot, then a solid slug into the boulders. The range was close enough so that either load might do damage.

"Stay down!" he snapped, and scrambled for the cover of a gully, keeping one eye on the boulders above.

He hadn't hoped to hit anything with his shots, only to keep the sniper pinned down until, Lord willing, he could get close enough for a clear target. A heavy-caliber bullet screamed overhead as he dived into the shelter of the gully. It looked like the sharpshooter didn't have any notions of changing positions for the moment.

Coming up on one knee, Stark threw another set of slugs and buckshot at the boulders. Then he rolled out of the gully and was up on his feet, running a zigzag course toward a low ridge. He threw himself the last few yards, landing on chest and forearms with a jolting impact. A small explosion of dirt erupted from the crest of the ridge inches above his head.

Stark rolled onto his back and wriggled sideways under cover of the ridge as he thumbed loads from his bandolier and jammed them into the shotgun. Reloaded, he dived over the ridge, rolled, and came up running, shotgun tilted up, firing from the hip.

He heard another shot from above but didn't know where the bullet went. He had gained a good distance by the time he took cover again. He was sweating, breathing hard, tasting grit in his teeth as he peered up at the hillside now looming close above him. His next spring should take him into the cover of the underbrush and stunted evergreens cloaking the grade.

Another blast from the buffalo gun tore down through the growth, but it was far wide of him. Maybe the rifleman was getting rattled. Stark sent some fire ripping back up through the growth in answer, reloaded, then gathered himself for another rush.

"Jim! He's running!" Prudence's shouted words reached him over the ringing in his ears. "That way!"

He flung a glance back at her, saw her exposing herself dangerously to point along the hill. Her position must've allowed her to see the enemy deserting his post under the fusillade of slugs and buckshot. Stark waved her frantically back under cover. As she obeyed, he straightened and moved at a crouching run in the direction she'd indicated, head turned to scan the grade above him.

He glimpsed a sinuous buckskinned figure darting through the brush a hundred yards up the slope. Skidding to a halt, he lifted the shotgun and tried to line it on the elusive form. He cut loose and knew he had missed as the sharpshooter disappeared. Instantly Stark rushed the hillside, scrambling several yards up its face. The buffalo gun boomed, but the shot came nowhere near. His opponent had lost track of him, Stark sensed.

He slowed his pace, striving for silence, working his way up the steep slope, staying to cover. Partway up he halted, listening intently. The sharp heady pulse of fear and danger coursed through him.

Had his enemy moved? Stark looked back toward where he'd left Prudence, hoping she might signal to him of the sniper's location. But the brush blocked his view of her vantage point.

Tensely he eased upward another few yards. He fancied he heard a rustling from above, but couldn't be sure. The repeated crashing of the heavy-bore weapons had silenced the normal bird calls of the woodlands. They had also, he thought sourly, probably carried across the plains to the approaching band of outlaws. He needed to finish this duel.

Blindly he fired uphill, swinging the shotgun in an arc, cutting loose a spread of three shots. Then he dropped flat, reloading with frantic haste. His opponent's response came within two seconds, shredding the leaves overhead.

Stark charged up the hill, closing on the source of the shot. Branches and brush tore at him; his booted feet scrabbled for purchase. He heard a startled yell of anger and frustration and glimpsed a flurry of movement up ahead and to his left. His wild charge had flushed his foe.

He flung himself aside and down, triggering the shotgun before he hit the ground. A roaring lance of flame answered him. On his side, he fired the remaining three loads from the shotgun, whipped out his Colt, and cocked back the hammer with a savage snap of his thumb.

He didn't pull the trigger.

The buckskinned figure he had seen earlier lurched out of the underbrush and tumbled sprawling downslope.

Catlike, Stark came erect. The body of the sharpshooter slid the last yard to stop almost at his feet. He couldn't tell how many of the shotgun's loads had hit him in that last fusillade.

Stark wasted no time on him. He stepped around the lifeless form and ascended to the thicket where the rifleman had been concealed. There was a trophy worth retrieving from this particular kill.

He found the Sharps in the brush where its owner must've dropped it when the loads from the shotgun caught him. It was an old piece, but well cared for, and it was undamaged. Stark returned to the sharpshooter and searched his body, coming up with only a handful of shells for the big rifle. Five in all. The rifleman had been running low on ammo. Still, five rounds was better than having an empty rifle.

He emerged into the open and waved. Below him he saw Prudence appear and return his wave with an eagerness she appeared to quell quickly. Using hand gestures, he directed her to get Red and bring him up. She hurried to obey.

How was she feeling now that he'd killed another man? Stark brooded. Even having accepted the need of it, he knew it would not sit well with her, and probably branded him irrevocably as a killer in her eyes.

He moved higher to a rocky promontory from which he could survey the grasslands. His mouth thinned, but he didn't feel much surprise at what he saw.

Within plain view of the naked eye, a group of horsemen were coming fast toward the hills, no doubt drawn by the sounds of the long-gun duel. Squinting, Stark was sure he spotted Garland himself at the head of the pack. Sunlight from the west glinted gold off his hair.

Stark made a rough count of about fifteen men. It was hard to be sure with the running horses moving beside and in front of one another. Heavy odds for a gunman and a lady lawyer with only one horse between them. Well—he hefted the Sharps—maybe he could lower those odds a little.

He found a likely boulder for a muzzle rest and knelt, laying the barrel across it. He fed one of the finger-long shells into the old gun and set the first trigger. Sleeving sweat from his forehead, he sighted down the length of the barrel at his target--Dirk Garland himself. Perhaps he could end things right here.

The range was long even for the Sharps, but he was unwilling to let them get much closer. Too, the late afternoon light was growing ever more uncertain.

He breathed out, set himself for the recoil, and adjusted the angle of the barrel by a trifle. At the squeeze of the trigger, the Sharps roared and bucked in his grip, the impact of its butt against his shoulder almost as if he'd gotten shot himself. He waved a hand to dissipate the billowing cloud of powdersmoke that obscured his vision and stung his eyes. Disappointment struck him like a blow.

Unhit, Garland had reined up in shock. The .50-caliber slug must've come close. But, firing an unfamiliar weapon, Stark hadn't been able to score a hit on the first try.

With fingers clumsier than he would've liked, he jammed another shell home. It was just dawning on Garland what was happening, but he was quick enough to react. He gestured at his men to scatter and put his mount forward in a switchbacking run.

Stark touched off the Sharps again. The horse of the man behind Garland dropped like a stone, its rider rolling clear, unhurt. Stark gritted his teeth in frustration. Three shells left, and he had yet to reduce the odds by even one.

He no longer had a clear shot at Garland. He chose another rider at random, and this time was heartened to see his target go backward off his horse as if he'd run into a tree limb at full gallop. The rest of the pack was scattered wide now, closing in on the broken ground bordering the hills.

He threw the last two shots while he still had targets, reloading and firing as quickly as he could. Both were misses.

Disgusted with himself and with the gun, Stark drew back from his sniper's rest. He had no more loads for the Sharps, so it would only be extra weight for him now. Of course, he acknowledged sourly, even having loads, he hadn't done much good with it. He dropped it into a rocky crevice in passing to keep it out of the hands of his foes. He didn't want it being used against him again.

The outlaws would be in the hills tomorrow. He

needed to round up Prudence and find a place to go to ground for the night. The owlhoots couldn't do much in the way of hunting them during the hours of darkness.

Morning would be a different story.

Chapter Thirteen

"Thanks," Stark said laconically. "You helped me out when you spotted that hombre making a run for it. I might not have gotten him if it hadn't been for you."

"Why do you do it?" Prudence asked softly after a moment. "Hire out your gun, I mean."

She was a dimly seen feminine presence seated close beside him in the secluded grassy draw where they had made their camp. Her knees were drawn tight to her chest. Night hung over the two of them.

"Because I'm good at it," Stark answered her.

"No, there's more to it than that," she persisted, and he sensed her turn her head to gaze at him, although his face would be unreadable in the darkness. "You've . . . you've devoted your life to it."

"Part of my life maybe."

"But why?"

Stark stared into the blackness. He had done his share of soul-searching over the years. For a God-fearing man to be in the trade he followed took some explaining, even to himself, at times.

"Why are you a lawyer?" he inquired at last.

"Because I like to help people."

"There's other ways to help folks besides arguing for them in a courtroom," he pointed out.

She shifted her position, drawing neither closer to nor farther from him. "I suppose I like the excitement of opposing other lawyers in the courtroom. And I want to be the best at what I do."

"There's your answer."

"But it's different," she protested. "I'm not risking my life."

"Some people need more help than they can get in a courtroom."

"That's what Marshal Nix and his deputies are for."

"I didn't see them helping you."

She pondered his answer—an attorney seeking a loophole in an opponent's argument. "I can't believe that you actually enjoy killing," she said at last.

"I don't," Stark replied flatly. "But I'm good at fighting. Most people get satisfaction out of doing what they're good at. Sometimes other people are hurt by what they do. The lawyer opposing you in the courtroom might not be able to feed his family if he loses to you. If he works for the prosecutor's office, he might be out of a job. And the damages the losing party has to pay in a civil suit might bankrupt him. But if what you're doing is in a good cause, those things shouldn't make you stop."

"There's still a difference," she objected.

"Yeah," said Stark, "there is."

He bestirred himself, rising to fetch their only bedroll from his saddle. He fancied he heard her softly indrawn breath as he moved away. "You better turn in." He tossed the bedroll easily in her direction. "I'm going to scout around a bit. I'll be back."

"What will we do tomorrow?" her quiet voice halted him.

He returned and stood towering over her seated form. She didn't move. He hesitated, then hunkered down beside her. He wasn't given to discussing his plans with others, but she had a right to know how things stood. And, he'd come to realize with some surprise, her persistent and challenging questions sharpened him, made him evaluate his plans a little more thoroughly and—maybe—improve them.

"We're pretty well trapped in these hills so long as we've just got one horse," he explained. "Heading cross-country would be a greenhorn's move. Garland would be sure to run us down. I located his camp when I went scouting earlier. After I figure they're bedded down, I'm going to try to get us a couple of their horses." He smiled. "I reckon a lawyer would call it horse theft."

"It's not funny," she spoke almost sharply. "You'll be in a great deal of danger."

"It's our best chance."

Her face was a pale lovely mask disturbingly close to his own. "Very well," she whispered.

Automatically Stark lifted a hand to brush his palm reassuringly across her cheek. She stiffened ever so slightly before his flesh could touch hers. He lowered his hand.

"I need to go take that look around," he said brusquely as he rose. "Go ahead and get some sleep."

"Wake me when you leave to take up horse stealing," she said softly, drowsiness already settling in her tones.

Stark slipped away. His quick reconnaissance of the area produced nothing to alarm him. From what he had seen of Garland's camp in the badlands, the outlaw chieftain was keeping his men loosely bunched for now. Stark doubted there would be any scouts roaming the hills. But it didn't pay to take chances with a shrewd opponent like Garland.

Stark returned to the draw and settled down a couple of yards from Prudence. She stirred but didn't awaken. Stark catnapped, rousing once when a raccoon trilled from a nearby tree. It was past midnight when he finally shrugged off the last vestiges of sleep.

He had already donned his Apache moccasins and replenished his bandolier with shotgun loads from his supply in his pack, so there were few preparations to make for his outing. He paused before touching Prudence's shoulder gently to awaken her.

"Get our gear together while I'm gone," he told her softly. "We may have to pull out fast when I get back."

"All right. Be careful."

There was a moment's hesitancy between them. Stark drew back. He heard her murmur something further in farewell as he left, but the words escaped him.

He moved through the darkness of the wooded hills by instinct, experience, and memory. A few years back, he had stalked a trio of cattle rustlers through this area, so this range wasn't entirely new to him.

From a vantage point on the edge of the hill country he looked down at Garland's camp. The outlaw had planned well, making his bivouac behind a low ridge for protection from any further sniper attacks. But the rough terrain would make it easier for a lone raider to approach undetected. Stark hoped Garland wouldn't be expecting the boldness of his ploy.

Face darkened by dirt, shotgun slung across his back, Stark came down out of the hills like a wraith. He slipped from one piece of cover to the next, staying low, keeping all his senses alert.

The horses were tied on the far side of the camp, at

the edge of the grasslands. Stark circled wide, skirting the camp itself. As he went to ground in a barren rocky draw, he heard the faint rasp of scales on stone as a good-sized snake retreated from his approach. He wondered if the irregular terrain of the badlands had magnified the noise to make the serpent sound that large.

Like the snake, he went on his belly once he was in the thick grass. He spotted one guard and went silently past him. Ahead he could see the dark shapes of the horses, hear their occasional movements, and smell their sweat-tinged scent. He halted and lay still, wondering at the absence of more lookouts.

Insects buzzed in the night. Bats whispered past overhead in darting pursuit of the bugs. A nighthawk called.

A man cleared his throat.

Stark's every muscle went taut. He had seen no sign of a second lookout. Where was the fellow?

"Hey, Zeke." The voice was a shouted whisper from about ten yards ahead. Apparently the speaker was concealed in the grass like Stark himself.

"Hush up, Perkins," a second voice warned from farther away. "You know what the boss said!"

"This is giving me the willies, laying out here in the grass, waiting for him to show up!" The first speaker ignored his companion's warning, although he kept his voice low enough so that it wouldn't carry far. "This jasper's bad medicine, I tell you. I done heard of him. Think of the way he killed Hollis. Looked like a cannon hit him. And he must've done for Buckskin too, and got his rifle. That was sure enough a Sharps he was using, and he didn't have one with him when he escaped with that woman. Had to be Buckskin's gun!"

"Shut up!" Zeke hissed urgently.

"Yeah, all right. But it wouldn't take much for me to pull up stakes and hightail it out of here!"

Having gotten his grousing out of his system for the time being, Perkins fell silent.

Stark stayed where he was, waiting and listening while he chewed on what he'd heard.

Garland had been expecting him to try for the horses! The cunning outlaw, schemer that he was himself, had set a trap for him, and he'd come precious close to walking—or rather crawling—into it. The warm night breeze seemed to have acquired a chill.

Stealing a couple of horses was not out of the question, Stark understood. Garland was too well prepared for such an effort. Even if he could reach the horses, he'd never get clear of the camp with one of them, much less two. The bitterness of defeat was galling.

But, he calculated, there still might be a way to gain something out of this mess, and maybe sow a little dissension among Garland's men at the same time.

Sliding the bowie from its scabbard, he wormed away from the unnerved Perkins toward the spot where Zeke's voice had sounded. He paused every couple of yards, and at last his nose caught the sweat, horse, and gun oil odors that betrayed Zeke's nearness.

Stark inched closer until he could make out a dim form hunkered down in the grass and hear the faint sounds of his prey's breathing. He was approaching from an angle, which was okay. A frontal attack would've been the most risky method.

Slowly, taking almost a full minute, Stark gathered himself, rising to one knee, his other leg outstretched behind him as though he was set to run a sprint. His fingers tightened around the worn hilt of the bowie.

Then, as Zeke's head started to turn toward the vague shape that had risen gradually up from the prairie, Stark lunged like a snake striking across the pair of yards separating them. The bowie—his fang—tore through fabric and into flesh. His left hand groped, then closed on Zeke's throat, clamping tight to stifle any outcry.

After a moment Stark eased himself off the lifeless form beneath him. There was no sound from Perkins. The noise of the brief scuffle had been lost in the vastness of the prairie, and now there was one less killer to dog their trail.

Stark crept away from the camp. A horse nickered behind him, probably at the scent of blood, but there was no alarm. Likely, Zeke's body would lie undiscovered until dawn.

Once clear of Perkins, Stark circled back toward the hills. It would've been a fool's play to try for another kill this night, particularly when he had no idea how many men Garland had posted to bushwhack him.

He ascended back up through the hills, weighing their choices. He could put Prudence on Red and have her strike out across the Lands on her own while he stayed behind to delay Garland and his crew. But, even if she would agree to such a strategy, it would leave her strictly on her own in a lawless realm where a lone woman, especially an attractive one, would be prize game for most anyone crossing her path.

"No luck," he reported tersely to her once he'd reached their camp. He didn't go into details. "Try to get some more sleep. We'll see how things look in the morning."

They didn't look good. Stark's field glasses showed him a lone horseman, just out of reach of a rifle, patrolling the plains to the east. He spotted another one to the south. With grim foreboding he knew there would likewise be men stationed at the other points of the compass. Garland had cordoned off the range of hills, knowing his prey to be holed up there. In the daylight it would be all but impossible to set out across the grasslands without being spotted by one of the outlaws on patrol.

Which left Garland with about a dozen men to scour the hills and root them out of hiding, Stark concluded grimly. Those dozen men, armed and alert, would be spreading out even now.

Stark explained as much to Prudence. "I'm going to put you somewhere safe, then do my best to discourage them," he finished.

She drew a ragged breath, as if coming to some momentous decision. "Is there any way I can help?"

"Thanks, but the answer's no. I'll need to move fast, and I can't afford to look out for anybody but myself."

"I want to help," she insisted.

"You'll help best by staying out of it," Stark said firmly enough to cut off any more argument.

From his prior days in these hills, he recalled a rock overhang, the mouth of which was concealed by dense brush. Beneath the overhang was a small chamber that could be reached only by negotiating a jumble of rubble and boulders that had fallen from the roof in past ages.

He located it with little trouble. The interior was cool and damp. Prudence shivered as she looked about.

"You'll be safer here than anywhere else I know of in this range," Stark told her. "I'll leave you my lantern from my gear, but don't light it unless you have to. Let me see your gun."

She pulled it from her waistband and passed it to him, their hands brushing in the exchange. Stark checked the weapon in the dim light, then handed it back. "Don't use it except as a last resort."

"I won't," she promised.

"Keep quiet and don't do anything to draw attention to yourself."

She gave a short nod of understanding, and Stark realized he was prolonging their separation with simple instructions he had no real need to give.

He stepped away from her. "So long. May be a spell before I come back."

"Watch yourself," she said simply.

Stark crawled back out through the boulders and made his way past the screen of underbrush. He took a moment to conceal signs of their entry, then legged it to Red where he'd tied the sorrel nearby.

The cold will to survive was rising in Stark as he rode out. He'd run and hid long enough. Now it was time to fight.

He headed for higher ground, riding carefully, at times leaving Red and scouting ahead on foot. He chose what looked to be the tallest hill in the range and kept steadily in that direction, checking his backtrail every few yards.

It was as he glanced back one of those times that he glimpsed a lone horseman skirting the edge of a clearing below him on a neighboring hill. Stark held Red motionless and used his field glasses. He recognized one of Garland's owlhoots riding upslope, seemingly headed for the same vantage point he himself had chosen.

It made sense, he reasoned. Garland would've wanted a lookout commanding the high ground. As on the night before, he might even have anticipated Stark's movements.

Stark ran his gaze over the contours of the terrain separating him from the other rider. Then he turned Red and nudged him on, slanting across the wooded face of the hill, staying always to cover so as not to carelessly reveal himself as the outlaw had done.

He caught one more glimpse of the fellow through an intervening screen of trees and estimated where he'd intercept the other's path. Dismounting, he crept the last fifty yards to the edge of a small clearing. The ground was reasonably level at this point on the grade. If possible, he wanted to keep from throwing any lead. Gunfire would only betray his position before he'd had the

chance to make use of the hilltop both he and his prey
were seeking.

Stark readied himself as he heard the nearing thud of
hoofbeats. In a moment the outlaw broke from cover,
staying close to the trees on the far side of the clearing.
He looked alert. Given a chance, he'd be ready enough
for trouble.

Stark didn't give him much chance. He erupted out of
the brush, having space for three hard running strides
across the clearing, before he left the ground in a high
twisting leap. In midair his foot shot out, driving solidly
into the rider's ribcage. The startled horse darted from
between them as his rider was literally kicked out of the
saddle. Landing on his feet, legs flexing to take the impact, Stark lunged forward. His bowie was in his hand.
He flung himself upon the fallen owlhoot and rose a
handful of seconds later, peering warily about.

The horse had pounded away through the woods.
Stark let it go. He retreated quickly from the exposed
clearing. He retrieved Red and ascended the rest of the
way up the hill. Leaving Red below the crest, he worked
his way through a tangle of brush to the summit, then
used his glasses to survey the surrounding hills.

He took his time, covering each piece of the countryside with deliberate care, careful to keep the lenses
shaded to prevent any betraying reflection. In all, he
spotted a half-dozen men. He knew there had to be
more—he estimated at least another five or six. But
some of them would be invisible in the thick growth and
rough terrain. Given all day, Stark suspected he could've
spotted every one of them. But he didn't think he had
all day. They were hunting for him too.

Garland wasn't among the searchers he spotted. Four
of them were working in pairs on horseback. The other
two, covering rougher ground, were on foot. From their
locations, he suspected Garland, like a military com-

mander, had assigned specific searchers to specific areas. The outlaw leader was again proving himself a wily and dangerous adversary. Stark was beginning to understand how he had been able to successfully elude capture and finally retire after years in the owlhoot trade.

Stark concentrated on the two closest horsemen. Old pros, they were riding together, separated a piece, but close enough to cover one another. Taking them by surprise wouldn't be easy. Watching their progress, Stark settled on a clump of outthrusting boulders a good distance ahead of them. Hoping they'd stay on their present route, he returned to Red.

The range of hills was big enough for a man to lose himself in for a spell, but eventually he would be rooted out by determined searchers. Stark did his best to lose himself as he traveled. He stuck to the draws between hills, emerging from the timber only when necessity demanded it. His nerves sang with tension. At any moment he expected a bullet from some unseen rifleman to slam into his body.

He had lost track of the two owlhoots by the time he gained the clump of boulders. Had they already passed by? he wondered. After five minutes of eyeballing the terrain he let his breath out in satisfaction as he spotted them emerging into view some hundred yards downslope from his position.

They were wending their way through the trees, still covering one another. Stark knew there was a good chance they'd spot him when they passed by below. He eased himself down even farther between the boulders, cutting off his view of the pair. He would have to wait until after they were past, which would cut down his chances of getting them both.

Hardly breathing, thinking of himself as a part of the rocks themselves, he lay there. Faintly came the sounds of the approaching riders. They grew louder, then began to diminish.

A darkness settled over Stark's soul. Briefly an image of Prudence McKay's solemn features flashed in his mind's eye. He put it aside. These hombres weren't asleep, either. They were out to kill him. Now wasn't any time for mercy.

In a single coordinated movement, he came up on one knee, shotgun to his shoulder, swinging it into line with the nearest target almost by instinct. The blast of buckshot ripped the outlaw from the saddle. Instantly Stark shifted the barrel, setting it on the second horseman as soon as he spotted him in the trees two dozen yards distant. He saw the owlhoot's arm coming up, pistol already in hand in the same second that his horse, spooked by the first shot, pitched under him. Stark cut loose with the shotgun. The heavy slug missed the figure atop the sidestepping horse. The outlaw's shot was wild and unaimed.

Stark levered and fired in a clocktick, and this time the spreading charge of buckshot tore through trees and underbrush and toppled the rider from his panicked horse.

The echoes bounced off the hills and died. Both horses had disappeared. Neither outlaw moved. Somewhere, foolishly, a man shouted an inquiry. There was no answer.

Stark's eyes narrowed. Silently he shifted his position, retreating a bit higher up the grade. Patiently he then settled down to wait some more.

Chapter Fourteen

Every time the muffled sound of distant shots reached her ears, Prudence shuddered. She felt tired and soiled. Her imagination pictured the dank gloom of her refuge with haunting images of Jim Stark lying dead or wounded in some remote part of the hills. He was one man against an entire gang. What could even he hope to accomplish?

She prayed for his safety and realized in the process that his death would mean something more to her than simply the loss of a protector. Just how much more she wasn't certain, and her mind shied away from the question that her jumbled emotions insisted on thrusting upon her.

By his own admission he was a man of violence—something she abhorred even while acknowledging the occasional need for violence to oppose lawlessness and anarchy. But he was also a man bound by strong moral codes that amazingly, seemed to mirror her own in some ways.

Her forced intimacy with him during their escape and flight had been disturbing, but in a way far different from the terror she had experienced while in the hands of the outlaws. Jim—when had she started thinking of him by such familiar terms?—had shown her only the courtesy and respect due and proper between a man and a woman in such circumstances.

Had she wanted him to do more? A foolish question here and now, she told herself, and one to which the answer must certainly be in the negative. Even though he had many admirable, even attractive, qualities to him, his violent trade stood as an unbreakable barrier between them. Yes, violence might sometimes be necessary, but she could never approve of him making it his profession. But still, his easy competence, the image of his chiseled features and broad shoulders, and the memory of the way his gray eyes seemed to grip and hold her hovered tantalizingly in her mind.

Outside the rocky chamber where she huddled, a horse snorted.

Involuntarily Prudence pressed her shoulders more tightly against the stone at her back. Its dampness had become icy. Jim had ridden out on Red, she knew. Was this him returning?

"Shut up, you sorry nag," a man's coarse voice rasped. "What're you carrying on about?"

This wasn't Jim, she realized with growing dread. This was one of Garland's men, and his horse, maybe scenting Red's earlier presence, had reacted as it passed near the brush concealing her sanctuary.

Silence. Prudence scarcely dared breathe. Her ears, their perception heightened by fear, caught the creak of saddle leather as though the rider was shifting his weight to gaze about.

She heard him grunt. ''Blamed if it don't look like there could be a hidey-hole back in there behind all that brush,'' he said then, talking to himself, or maybe to his horse.

Wordlessly Prudence prayed.

''As good a place to light down for a spell as any, I reckon,'' came his voice. Prudence could tell when he dismounted. He muttered something crude about riding horses up and down mountains all day.

With sweating palms Prudence withdrew the revolver from her waistband. She realized she had stopped breathing, and for an awful straining instant she was unable to get her lungs to work again. She gripped the gun so tightly that it trembled in her fists.

Boots crunched in the brush. The outlaw let out another grunt; this one may have been in surprise. What had he seen? She pictured him, and crude and uncouth, advancing slowly into the undergrowth, peering ahead with evil suspicious eyes.

She put both thumbs over the hammer of the revolver. If he discovered the hidden chamber, she would be cornered. There was no other way out save through the nest of boulders.

There was more thrashing in the brush, more grunts of surprise of discovery. Slowly her thumbs eased the hammer back. The click of it coming to half-cock was muffled, but it crashed like thunder in her ears.

''Well, I'll be hanged!''

The exclamation told her he had spotted the jumble of rocks, and, most likely, the blackness of the niche behind them. He would be helpless when he dropped to his knees to crawl into the niche, she calculated. That would be the moment when she had to use the revolver, before he had a chance to spot her and get his bearings. If she gave him that chance, she would almost certainly end up at his mercy just as she and Jim might've ended up at the mercy of all the outlaws, she realized suddenly, if he hadn't kicked a sleeping man, and shot another from ambush. . . .

She had no time to ponder the revelation. A pebble, tossed from outside, rattled across the stone floor. Prudence let out a tiny startled cry, and her fingers tightened convulsively on the trigger. Only the half-cock of the hammer kept her from firing. She bit down hard on her lip in remorse, the sudden hammering of her heart seeming to echo in the tiny chamber.

"That you in there, girlie?" The outlaw's coarse tones confirmed her worst fears. Like a seasoned hunter trying to flush his prey, he had thrown a stone into the den to get her to betray herself.

She bit her lip even harder, refusing to respond again. She couldn't resist scrabbling sideways along the wall in a futile effort to put herself farther from the mouth of the chamber.

"I hear you moving around in there, honey. Who'd of thought, with all these fellows looking for you, it'd be old Harry himself who found you? Must be, you're alone in there, else that Peacemaker fellow would've ventilated me for sure by now." He laughed heavily. "What about it, hon? You going to come out for old Harry?"

Remotely Prudence realized he was talking in order to further demoralize her. It was working. Her teeth were trying to chatter, and she clamped them so tightly together it hurt her jaws.

A bizarre, grotesque sound filtered into the chamber. Her persecutor was whistling! It was a carefree, jovial tune that grated on her nerves like sandpaper, exactly as it was no doubt supposed to do.

A spark of rebellion stirred amid her fear. In the courtroom, smarter men than this thug had tried to unnerve her and had failed. She realized Harry plainly didn't believe her to be armed. She looked down at the gun in her trembling hands, and set her jaw. Just as opposing lawyers had learned to their grief that she was well armed with legal skills and knowledge, so Harry might learn she was well armed in this arena also.

The whistling broke off. "No need of me calling anyone else just yet, hon," he advised. "You're a mighty pretty thing. If you was to come on out, nice-like, you and me could have us a little hoedown of our own. Then, maybe, if you're real sweet, I could see about getting you away from Dirk. Why, you and me could have a high old time in some of those towns back over the border. What about it, honey?"

Prudence didn't answer. The images his crude words conjured up were appalling. Briefly she considered emptying the gun through the entryway in the hopes of hitting him. She discarded the notion. Jim Stark would've called it a greenhorn's move.

"I'm getting mighty impatient," Harry's voice sounded again. "How's about if I just lit a little old match to this underbrush out here? How'd you like that, huh?" It's mighty dry—should burn real nice. You'd be like some varmint getting smoked out of its den. Be a lot easier on you if you'd come on out now."

Prudence swallowed hard. If he fired the scrub brush, the chamber would be filled with smoke. In its close confines, she'd face suffocation unless she went out into his clutches. Her mind raced as furiously as it had ever done in any court proceeding. If Harry was a hostile witness on the stand, she would try to lure him into making an admission against interest, lure him into a trap. Maybe she could use her verbal skills to lure Harry into a different kind of trap.

"I'm lighting the match, honey!"

"Wait!" Prudence called, and the involuntary tremor in her voice only made it sound all the more authentic.

"Please, don't. I'm . . . I'm hurt. I can't come out by myself."

A long pause ensued. "Now, you don't expect old Harry to swallow that, do you?"

"It's true," she insisted, desperation giving her lie the sound of truth. "I fell and broke my leg. Mr. Stark had to leave me here while he went for help."

She could imagine Harry mulling it over in his dull mind. "Just crawl on out," he encouraged at last. "I'll give you a hand."

"I can't. You'll have to carry me." That image should get his mind working, she thought.

"I can't carry you out of there!" he objected.

"Yes, you can! Mr. Stark carried me in. There's plenty of room. Oh, please hurry! It hurts so much!"

She continued to plead with him, using persuasive techniques to which she never would've stooped in the courtroom. All the time she was aware of the slow passage of minutes that increased the likelihood of another outlaw happening by.

But at length the notion of a helpless woman trapped in a hidden chamber was too much for Harry to resist.

"Hold on, honey! I'm coming!"

She heard him thrashing through the brush, saw his shadow darken the cave's entrance. Numbly she pulled the hammer of the gun all the way back to full cock.

Harry was grunting and snorting as he got down on his knees and started to crawl through the narrow passage. Prudence waited until his body had blocked the entrance, and the dark bulky shape of his head and shoulders was emerging into the chamber. Then, hating what she had to do, she closed her eyes and pulled the trigger. The recoil jerked her arms up. Blindly she lowered the gun and cocked and fired again. Harry screamed. The reverberations in the tiny chamber deafened her like palms clapped over her ears.

She opened her eyes to the tearing bite of gunsmoke, just in time to glimpse her target lurching back clear of the entrance. He collapsed with one hand still extended into the chamber.

Prudence sat there, too stunned and afraid to move, until the hanging powdersmoke drew a rasping cough from her throat. Harry was dead, she understood. He hadn't moved. But his body was lying outside the cavern and might be visible to any of his cohorts who happened along. The idea of drawing him farther into the niche was unbearable. She would have to get out past him and somehow conceal his body.

The horrible task of pushing his bulk clear of the passage so she could emerge was the stuff of fevered nightmares, but she managed it. Sweating and shaky, she rose at last to her feet in the daylight and looked frantically about for some way to hide his body. His poking and thrashing in the brush had left irrevocable signs of his presence. Had the shots been heard? she wondered as she moved clear of the overhang.

"What's all the shooting about, Harry? Why, what the devil?"

Prudence spun about to see the mounted figure that had just appeared. Harry hadn't been riding alone! Noticing his absence, his cohort must've come back to check on him. And it was too late to hide; she had already been seen.

She took a faltering step back, staring down at her empty hands with the harrowing recollection that she had dropped the gun inside the cavern as she struggled to dislodge the body. She cast a frantic look at the overhang, preparatory to turning and fleeing for its sanctuary. As if reading her mind, the horseman kicked his mount into a quick spurt that put him between her and the mouth of the cave.

Astride his horse he loomed over her like a centaur,

unshaven and totally disreputable, a barbaric gleam in his eyes.

"Well, looky, looky here," he drawled with immense, evil satisfaction.

"I tell you, I've had my bellyfull of this," the outlaw named Perkins said with feeling, shifting his horse about in an uneasy circle. "Both of them are dead. Shot right off their horses, it looks like. We're supposed to be hunting him, but he's the one hunting us!"

"So what are you planning to do?" his companion drawled.

"I'm giving some serious thinking to hauling tail out of these hills and not looking back!"

"Garland wouldn't cotton to that." The other outlaw spat tobacco juice.

"I don't ever plan to cross trails with Dirk Garland again, once I'm clear of this sorry mess," Perkins declared flatly. "It was bad doing's when I joined up with your crew. I know about this Peacemaker. It means big trouble when he gets your scent. I never counted on tangling with him!"

"You ain't tangled with him yet," his compadre pointed out.

"Yeah, but I got an ugly feeling that tells me I will if I stay in these parts much longer. Why, he might be aiming at us over his shotgun barrel right now!"

The idea seemed to shake the other outlaw's confidence a bit. He cast about with shifting eyes. "From the looks of them two, we'd be dead if he was."

"That's what I'm talking about!" Perkins said insistently. "He's like some blamed haint or something waiting to get us when we ain't looking. He killed Zeke with that bloody big knife while Zeke was almost right next to me, and I never heard a thing. Could've been me just as easy. Or you."

"Maybe you're right." The outlaw's voice took on a musing tone. "We can't never go back to Kansas after this. Had it mighty good there. Dirk was a fool to give it up for a tinhorn scheme like this. That son of his is no-account worthless. Seems stupid to maybe get killed over him. Yeah, I reckon I'm with you, Perkins. Let's ride while we got the chance!"

As the two outlaws turned their horses hurriedly down the grade, Stark lowered the shotgun he had kept trained on them during their confab. He watched their departure, and some of the sour taste left by the ambush killings of the past twenty-four hours faded from his mouth.

How many were left to account for? He ran a mental tally. Garland, Wilson, and Shed—the most dangerous ones—were still at large, along with maybe another two or three hombres. He figured he could disregard the outlying scouts who were patrolling the perimeter of the hills. With things turning against their cohorts, they'd be unlikely to take a hand.

He had been long enough in one place. He returned to Red and descended into a sandy winding gully that led him generally toward a tall hill he had earmarked. Not as high as the other hill he had used earlier as a lookout point, it still would command a good view of part of the range, maybe enabling him to spot Garland himself or one of his remaining followers.

A gleam of white in the dirt wall of the gully caught his searching eye. He reined up as he realized the skull of some large animal was partially embedded there. An empty eye socket above a curving sweep of ivory stared at him. It was a bison, he understood, but not one of the breed that still lurked in small numbers in remote parts of the grasslands. This, he recognized, was of a variety that had roamed these plains centuries before. He had seen illustrations of them; they had been larger, with more massive horns, than their descendants.

As he looked closer, he saw a flint arrowhead embedded in the skull. And all along a six-yard section of the bank he saw pieces and fragments of other bones and skulls exposed. An ancient bison kill, he surmised with a sense of awe, buried by the debris of centuries. How long had the silent bones been here? he wondered as he rode slowly past. An iciness touched his spine. Unless he rode mighty careful, his own bones might litter these hills a century from now.

He edged Red around a mass of dead brush and fallen limbs that had accumulated during high rains at a narrow spot in the draw. Then his senses heightened as he saw booted footprints crossing the gully ahead of him. The boots were big. Their wearer had scrambled up out of the draw and apparently ascended a steep grade that would've baffled a horse. The tracks had been made within the past half hour.

Leaving Red in the gully, Stark crossed a grassy open space to the foot of the grade. Tipping the brim of his Stetson back, he peered up through the trees and undergrowth clinging to the slope. There was no sign of the climber. Stark leaned sideward for a different angle of view.

The rifle shot roared from behind him, and the bullet, zipping past his head, buried itself in the grade with a miniature eruption of dirt.

Stark flung himself prone in the sparse shelter of a shallow defile at the base of the slope. Three more bullets chopped into the dirt just above his lowered head.

''Throw out your guns and I'll take you alive,'' an unfamiliar voice called. ''The boss will be wanting to know where you got the girl hid out.''

Lying flat on his belly, head burrowed into his arms, Stark knew he didn't have a choice. There'd been no chance to return fire. This yahoo, whoever he was, had him cold.

"All right," he called. "I'm getting up."

"Stay down till you've shucked them shooters!" The tone of voice didn't brook disobedience.

Awkwardly Stark tossed his shotgun in the direction of the voice. He followed it with his Colt. Neither weapon discharged. From the edge of his vision, he tried to spot the rifleman, but the fellow was well hidden. His voice put him somewhere across the sandy gully. Likely he'd been paired up with the man who'd ascended the grade, and had lagged behind him as they'd hiked the rough terrain.

"Wilson mentioned that hideout gun," the voice called. "Throw it out too."

Stark complied. He'd been stripped of all his firearms, while his captor, at the very least, was packing a rifle. Stark saw him step into the open and come to the edge of the draw. Its twelve-foot gap kept him from coming any closer for the moment.

"Get up and put your arms over your head."

Stark pushed himself to his knees. He was in the shade of the hill rising above him, and he prayed his movements would be partially hidden. As he rose, turning his body so the motion would be concealed, he pulled the bowie, manipulating it like a sleight-of-hand artist so the heavy blade rested along the inside of his forearm. When he straightened and turned to face his captor, arms upraised, he held the hilt in his right hand, arm turned inward, the blade lying along the inside of his forearm.

The rifleman gripped his weapon alertly at waist level. Stark, arms held high, went toward him, calculating the space separating them. The outlaw's eyes narrowed suspiciously as he saw the odd positioning of Stark's arm.

"I hurt my arm," Stark said smoothly, still moving forward.

The outlaw hesitated, and at that instant Stark reached the exact spot marking the distance he wanted between them. He stopped abruptly and twirled the bowie deftly so the blade pointed skyward. His right arm swung back, then forward, in a circular sweep, the hilt of the knife sliding smoothly from his grasp. The bowie spun through the air, and the rifleman reeled backward and collapsed with the big blade embedded in him.

Stark drew in air and straightened slowly from his follow-through. Throwing a bowie was tricky even from the proper distance, and especially against an armed opponent who, given the chance, could squeeze a trigger faster than a knife could fly.

He heard the heavy pound of feet and a grunt of effort, and started to turn just as Shed's lowered shoulder hit him from behind like the butting head of one of the ancient bison he'd seen entombed in the gully wall. He was flung sprawling, and Shed's trampling feet were suddenly coming at him.

Instinct made him roll so that the brawler's boot raised a puff of dust as it smashed down where his skull had been only an instant before. Again the booted foot drove down for him, but this time he got his hands up to catch it, his arms flexing back until his elbows touched the ground beneath the force of the driving stomp. He was all but pinned like a snake beneath a bootheel.

But this snake could bite. Stark hammered the heel of his moccasin against the knee of Shed's anchor leg. Then he twisted his lower body and twined his own legs about Shed's legs. He gave a straining flex of his body, and a thrust of his arms that brought Shed crashing to the ground.

Stark scrambled to regain his feet. Bruised, half-winded, he could only guess that Shed, returning from having scaled the hill, had seen the chance to blindside him and taken it.

The burly outlaw bounded back to his feet almost as quickly as Stark. He was agile for all his bulk. His lips peeled back to show the hole left by his missing tooth. He didn't look to be too bothered by the death of his comrade.

"Finally ran you to ground, Stark," he enthused. "Been wanting to get my hands on you when you weren't packing all them guns and that pigsticker." He gave a shake of his shaggy head, like a bull getting ready to charge. "I'm fixing to pound you till you tell me where that little lawyer gal is. Then I think I'll break your arms and legs and leave you to wriggle out of these hills on your belly." He dropped one meaty hand to his pistol, pulled it from its holster and tossed it carelessly aside. "Don't want you to go getting no ideas about maybe pulling my own gun and using it on me." His grin was ugly.

Stark had been considering exactly that. He didn't have time to fool with this bruiser on his own bare-knuckle terms.

But it didn't look like he had much choice.

"Come on." Shed motioned him forward. "Let's see if you're as good without them guns as with them!"

Stark did his best to show him. He slid in fast, his knee rising, then his leg straightening to drive the sole of his foot full into Shed's midriff. He skipped back, a little surprised that Shed only grunted beneath the impact.

"So, you're one of them fellows who likes to use his feet. I tangled with a Frenchman who pulled tricks like that." Shed's grin was devilish. "I broke his leg before I gave him a taste of my boots."

Fists up, he was moving in before he finished speaking, and he watched Stark's feet warily. Stark raised his fists also, holding them in front of him at head level. He jerked a knee up in a feint to draw Shed's eyes, then went in fast again. His left fist shot out in a straight jab to Shed's face; his right uppercut twice to his jaw in a half second's time. Stark spun to the outside, cocked his leg, and flicked his foot out sideward to land it under Shed's ribcage.

Shed whirled toward him. Stark had used fists and feet; now Shed would be on the lookout for both. And he didn't seem to be hurt at all. He let out a deep rumble and came at Stark with the force of an avalanche. Stark tried to wheel clear, but Shed, expecting it, swung a wide looping left that Stark had to backpedal to avoid. He recollected Garland saying Shed had nearly killed a prizefighter in a similar brawl. Schooled by bitter experience, Shed had his own brutally effective style of fighting.

He came sledging in with his big fists. Stark covered up, dropping an elbow to block a hooking left, snapping up a forearm to absorb the force of a murderous roundhouse. He felt the force of the thwarted punches all the way down through the soles of his feet. He kept on retreating, snapping kicks at Shed's knees and his legs, trying to slow him. But there was no chance to set himself properly, and Shed's legs were like tree trunks. Stark's kicks seemed to bounce harmlessly off.

Then a scything left got under Stark's guard, ripping the air from his lungs and bending his body sideways like a bow. Before he could recover, an overhand right crashed down on the juncture of neck and shoulder, hammering him to his knees. He flung his palms out to support himself. Both of Shed's mauling hands clamped around his vulnerable neck from above and closed like a hangman's noose.

Stark was on hands and knees in front of Shed, the air knocked out of him, his wind cut off. Shed's massive weight bore down on him. Desperately he groped behind his neck with a fumbling hand. His other arm trembled beneath the weight pressing down on him. Redness tinged his vision, and his whole skull pulsed. Then his searching fingers found the thumb of Shed's right hand. They peeled it free from its grip, tightened around it, then wrenched it backward.

Shed's howl rang like a blessing in Stark's ears. Rather than have his thumb dislocated, Shed yielded, releasing his grip to snatch his hand free. Stark twisted loose from his other hand and threw himself rolling clear of the knee Shed drove at his face. He came up on his feet to see Shed shaking his right hand, his face red with fury. Shed growled and lumbered in swinging.

New strength surged in Stark. He had escaped a hold that would've killed most men, and damaged one of his foe's hands in the process. And maybe Shed had felt the kicks to his legs after all, because now there was the slightest bit of an awkward shuffle to his gait.

Stark sucked in a draught of air and went to meet him, guard up, head and torso weaving. He dipped below Shed's first punch, uppercut to the brawler's belly, and wheeled clear, hooking a left to Shed's ear. He kept moving and bobbing, evading a few of Shed's blows, blocking and parrying others, punching in turn to head and body. Sometimes Shed's fists got through and rocked Stark, but the brawler was favoring his right hand a little and was not so quick on his feet, so that Stark could outmove and outpunch him most of the time.

Looking for his chance, Stark rapped his fist against Shed's injured right hand. Shed winced and actually flinched back. Baffled, panting, he came to a frustrated halt. Stark stepped closer and snapped his foot up and around at Shed's skull.

But Shed wasn't finished. Still fast, his hands shot up to clamp on Stark's ankle, and, even with a weakened hand, his grip was instantly numbing.

"Hah! Got you now!"

Shed wrenched the captured leg painfully, trying to tear it from its socket. Fear twisted Stark's gut as cruelly as Shed twisted his leg. He went with the movement, kicking off with his other leg, rotating his body in midair to drive his free foot against Shed's jaw with the whole rolling force of hips and body behind it.

The kick drove Shed's head swiveling sideward on his thick neck. He rocked back a step, his hands jumping free of Stark's ankle. Stark landed rolling and bounced up onto his feet. For not over two seconds Shed was stunned, his eyes glassy.

Before they cleared, Stark whirled toward him, lifting one straightened leg to bring it sweeping around in a full circle that connected with the side of Shed's skull like a swinging fence post. Shed reeled drunkenly. Stark slashed at him with both fists. Shed pivoted about beneath the impacts so that his back was to the edge of the gully some two yards behind him.

Stark retreated fast, took two running steps forward, and launched himself into the same leaping kick he had used to knock that other outlaw out of the saddle. His driving foot, backed by his full flying bulk, took Shed square over the heart, even as he tried to lurch aside. Arms flailing, Shed stumbled back and toppled into the gully.

Cautiously Stark approached the edge, stepping to one side before peering over. Shed lay crumpled on the gully floor. From the angle of his head, Stark could tell his neck had been broken in the fall. He didn't look to be breathing. The kick had probably killed him.

Hastily Stark collected his weapons. Garland and Wilson were still on the loose, and Prudence was still in danger. He had no time to spend recovering from the brawl.

As he slipped the hideout .38 into its holster, he stiffened tautly and turned. From the direction of the hidden cave came the rolling sounds of gunfire.

Chapter Fifteen

Desperate, Prudence tried to dodge behind the outlaw's horse to reach the sanctuary of the cave and the
pistol she had left there. But the owlhoot wheeled his
horse deftly, its shoulder brushing her with enough force
to fling her bruisingly to the ground. She scrambled to
regain her feet, catching a fragmented glimpse of the
owlhoot coming out of his saddle like a cowboy going
after a roped heifer. The next instant his lean hand
clamped on her wrist. She was yanked to her feet, her
arm twisted brutally until she was half doubled forward,
unable to move.

"Feisty little wildcat, ain't you?" her captor crowed.
"Well, I'm just the rounder who can tame you!"

"Take your hands off her, you cutthroat!"

The familiar voice, thundering its demand like an echo
out of the past, was so unexpected, so totally foreign to
this remote wilderness, that Prudence was momentarily
frozen in shock as her captor released her and wheeled

175

toward his challenger. Her startled eyes took in the daredevil figure of Temple Houston, long hair lifted by the breeze, coattails flipped back to reveal the pearl handles of twin pistols over which his hands hovered.

"Throw down your gun and surrender!" Houston barked.

Instead, the outlaw clawed for his revolver. Prudence darted clear. Still, she glimpsed Houston's hands swoop like diving hawks. Both his guns came up blasting fire. The owlhoot, his gun untriggered, spun beneath the impacts of the bullets and dropped in a lifeless sprawl.

For a moment Temple stood, smoking guns clenched in his fists. Then he strode forward as if embodying some paragon of justice, and halted over his victim. His handsome features were stern.

Abruptly he twirled his guns smoothly back into their holsters. His face relaxed some as he turned to Prudence. "Did he mistreat you?"

Prudence's voice caught in a little gasp. Quite involuntarily she ran to him and he drew her comfortingly to his chest. "Thank God you came!"

"Yes," he said.

She felt his encircling arm grow more possessive than protective, and, catching hold of her emotions, she put her palms against his chest and pushed herself free of his embrace. He didn't object.

"How did you get here?" Her bewilderment sounded in her tones.

"I got some leads on those brigands who abducted you. I was on their trail when I heard all the shooting from these hills. It sounded like a war, so I decided to check into it. I had to get the drop on some sorry villain out on the plains. He turned tail when I outdrew him."

"I thought you might be dead!"

"No, but that beating I took was the worst case of assault and battery that I ever care to be the victim of!"

He glanced about, right hand dropping to his pistol. "Where are the rest of them?"

"One's over there." She pointed at Harry.

For some reason she felt a trace of satisfaction in seeing Houston's eyes widen in surprise. "You did that?"

The satisfaction vanished. Despite herself, she shuddered. "Yes."

"And the others?"

"Jim . . . I mean, James, that is, Mr. Stark is after them."

"Stark!" Houston burst out. "How did he get mixed up in this?"

Briefly Prudence explained. Houston listened with growing amazement. "That's quite a tale," he commented when she finished.

"I don't know if Jim is still alive. He's been gone for hours."

"From what you've said, he may have his hands full. But he's a professional at this sort of thing. He can take care of himself. Right now, the first order of business is to get you out of these hills and head for civilization."

"No!" Prudence objected sharply. "I won't leave until I know what has happened to him!"

Houston opened his mouth as though to object in exasperation, but another voice cut him off: "Don't reckon neither of you folks are going nowhere just now. Drop the gun, tinhorn."

Houston was wheeling before the words were finished, his right hand coming up filled with his pistol. Prudence saw a blur of movement from the arm of one of the two figures who had stepped into view. The harsh crack of a shot sent Houston spinning sideways, clutching at his shoulder. Still on his feet, he froze, looking down the smoking barrel of Slick Wilson's revolver.

"Get rid of the other one, Mr. Fancy Dan," the gunfighter drawled easily. "You're mighty fast for a fellow dresses like a tenderfoot. I meant to kill you, and I will unless you do what I say.''

Grudgingly Houston complied with his order.

Prudence's spirit shrank within her as Dirk Garland swaggered past his hired gun and approached his captives. He was flushed, his yellow mane damp with sweat, but a cruel triumph gleamed in his eyes as they devoured Prudence.

He switched his gaze to Houston. ''Who the devil are you?''

The lawyer didn't answer. Prudence could sense his shame and anger. She found a moment to feel a deep sympathy for him.

Garland snorted derisively. ''Don't guess it matters none.''

''We need to get out of the open, Boss,'' Wilson suggested tensely. He had drawn near. His eyes seemed to be flicking in a dozen different directions at once.

Some of the triumph faded from Garland's manner. He glanced nervously about. ''Where's Stark?'' he demanded harshly of Prudence.

Her heart leaped. Jim wasn't dead! Or at least, she amended, if he was, Garland didn't know of it. She squared her shoulders. ''I'm sure I don't know.''

Garland snarled and lifted an arm as if to backhand his knuckles across her face. Houston growled. Prudence stood firm.

''He's somewhere close, Boss; I can feel it,'' Wilson advised in low tones. ''He's been on our tail almost since we heard the shots and started in this direction. You should've let me stay behind and face him straight up like I wanted.''

Garland lowered his threatening arm. ''That beggar's killed enough of my men,'' he growled. ''Didn't want to risk losing you.''

''I can take him!'' Wilson insisted in a tone so cold

and intense that it slid ice down the back of Prudence's neck.

"Forget it. I got a better idea." Garland's long arm snaked out and snagged Prudence's wrist. She gasped as he yanked her against his broad chest. She caught a whiff of the foul odor of his furred vest as he spun her so he held her before him.

Houston shifted, but subsided beneath the threat of Wilson's gun.

"Stark!" Garland's deafening shout rang in Prudence's ear. "Wilson says you're out there! If so, then you can hear me."

His words echoed into unbroken silence. Wilson shifted closer to Garland. Prudence realized they were both using her as a shield. Outrage stiffened her, but Garland's arm tightened like an iron bar.

"Sing out, blast you!" Garland thundered. "I got the girl. No chance you can get her away from me this time!"

Still only silence greeted his shouted words.

"All right, so you don't want to palaver! Well, I'll give you just one more chance! Show yourself, or I'll get awful cussed mean with this little filly! Her daddy will still be wanting her back, even if she's a mite soiled!" Tension rang shrill in his voice.

Was Jim out there in the brush? Prudence questioned silently in an agony of hope and fear. Was he nearby and watching? What choice did he have but to comply with Garland's demands?

"Wilson!" Jim Stark's voice rang out as though in answer to her questions.

The gunman glanced briefly at his chief, then called in reply, "I'm listening!"

"You and me got some unfinished business between us. Gun business."

Wilson licked his thin lips. "Yeah," he shouted, "we do!" The echoes of his voice faded.

"How about we finish it now?" Stark's tones came back. "Straight up, face-to-face, like you wanted."

"You serious?" Wilson demanded.

"I'm serious."

Again Wilson cut a look at Garland.

"Get him out in the open!" the outlaw leader ordered softly. "We'll both get the drop on him!"

It was to be a trap, Prudence understood with horror. Once Jim showed himself, he'd have no chance against these ruthless killers. She opened her mouth to cry out a warning, but, as if guessing her intent, Garland shifted his arm to her throat, cutting off her words under brutal pressure. With his free hand he drew his gun and pressed its cold muzzle against her temple.

"It's a deal, Stark!" Wilson hollered. "Come out with your hands empty!" He holstered his own gun.

"No tricks or I blow the girl's head off!" Garland added.

Prudence saw that Temple Houston had sunk to his knees, one hand still clamped to the wound in his shoulder. His face was pale, his expression vague. He appeared on the verge of losing consciousness.

Prudence's spirit faltered with hopelessness as Jim Stark stepped into the open.

Temple Houston was out of this fight, Stark assessed coldly. He didn't know how the gunslinging lawyer had come to be here. It didn't matter. His focus had to be on the pair of outlaws and their hostage.

"You're a blamed fool, Stark!" Garland shouted, and jerked his pistol away from Prudence's head to aim it squarely at him past her shoulder.

"No!" Slick Wilson's left hand shot over to grip Garland's arm and thrust it upward before his finger could pull the trigger. The gunman's face bore a feral savagery. "He's mine! Like I told him! I mean it, Dirk!"

"You've gone loco, Slick!" Garland protested, but he didn't try to cross his segundo any further. "Go ahead and have your fool shoot-out. I'm keeping the girl right here."

Wilson released his arm and stepped clear, careful to stay out of reach of Houston. The gunslick's face looked older than ever, skin tight as stretched leather, lips peeled back with an unholy hunger. The fingers of his gunhand opened and closed mechanically.

Stark had left his shotgun behind. There had been no way to use it with Prudence so close to the two men. His challenge to Wilson had been a desperate ploy that might still end up in getting him and Prudence both killed.

He advanced a bit, eyeing the gunfighter warily. "Time to find out if you've still got it, Wilson."

"Yeah," Wilson said, and his hand flashed for his gun.

Stark pulled the Peacemaker with a lightning flex of his arm that brought it up and level and firing a half-breath before Wilson's gun discharged. Wilson rocked backward, his gun hand wobbling. Stark shot him again, more carefully this time, and his legs gave way.

As the gunman fell Stark ducked and swiveled toward Garland. A bullet whipcracked past him. Prudence was fighting the outlaw's grip; her thrashing and Stark's movement had spoiled Garland's shot. Weaving, Stark tried to line his Colt, but the struggling pair gave him no target.

Garland's gun roared again as Prudence shoved his arm aside. Garland spat a frustrated curse and thrust Prudence from him, his long pelt of hair swinging. Before he could get his gun centered, Stark shot him in his lionskin vest, and put another bullet on top of the first for good measure.

Garland dropped to his knees. He was still glaring, still trying to continue the fight, when he fell forward on his face and lay still. Stark spared a glance for Wilson. The gunfighter had gotten his answer, he mused ruefully. He didn't need to check further to be sure both men were dead.

Prudence was picking herself up from the grass. Houston was staring at him through pain-dulled eyes. Automatically Stark began to reload the Peacemaker.

"Obliged for the help, Houston," Stark said. He hunkered down next to where the lawyer sat leaning against a convenient boulder, his arm in a sling. The words had come out more stiffly than he'd planned.

"From what I saw, you didn't need any help," Houston said in jaundiced tones. "I do wish I could've gotten my hands on one of them in particular, though. Big fellow. Punched like a prizefighter. Know who I mean?"

"That'd be Shed."

"The name fits. Any idea what became of him?"

"Fell and broke his neck."

Houston's eyes narrowed. "You have a hand in it?"

"More like a foot."

Houston settled his shoulders back against the boulder. His gray eyes flashed with frustration. "You're just a regular ring-tailed hellion, ain't you, Peacemaker?" he said with an edge of bitterness. "Take on the whole gang, rescue the girl, and walk away without a scratch."

"Grace of God one of them didn't get me before I got them."

Houston's lip curled. "That's a mighty odd attitude for a mercenary."

Stark nodded at his pearl-handled revolvers. "Mighty odd gear for a shyster."

* * *

"Temple, are you feeling better this morning?" Prudence had emerged from the makeshift tent Stark had rigged for her. She looked fresh and appealing, already well on her way to recovering from her ordeal.

Stark rose as she approached. She spared him a brief smile before kneeling next to Houston to fuss with his sling.

"I'm fine," Houston said with a growl. "It was just a crease." He used his good arm to push himself to his feet. His mouth thinned in pain, but he made no sound. He shot Stark a challenging look.

"Can you ride?" Prudence demanded with an undertone of irritation.

Houston caught himself and flashed her a charming smile that must've cost him an effort. "I'm certain I'll be able to sit a horse. A day's rest has done wonders for me. And I trust you're feeling better?" The irritable gunman had been smoothly replaced by the suave gentleman.

"Much better, thank you," Prudence told him.

Houston looked past her to Stark. "What about it, my good man? Did you find traces of any of the brigands still prowling these hills when you went scouting yesterday?"

"Nope," Stark drawled heavily. "Reckon they've all hightailed it, pard."

Prudence shuttled puzzled eyes back and forth between them. Stark wheeled and strode away. He fancied he heard the murmur of their voices behind him.

They had spent two nights and a day at their campsite, well removed from the scene of the last violent showdown. Houston had needed time to recover before riding much, and Stark had wanted a chance to check on the remaining members of the outlaw gang.

He was cinching his saddle a little tighter when he

sensed her presence behind him. He gave an extra tug that brought an unhappy snort from Red before he turned to face her.

She gestured at the horses. "Are they ready?"

Stark nodded. He wondered where Houston was lurking.

"How long will it take us to reach Guthrie?" she asked.

"A few days. We'll get word to your father as soon as possible."

She nodded absently, then drew a deep breath. "So . . . what will you do when we get back?"

Stark hitched a shoulder in a half-shrug. "Make my report to Blaine, then see if anybody else is looking to hire my services."

"James Stark: Peacemaker for Hire?" she said with an ironic bite to her words.

"Prudence McKay, Attorney and Counselor at Law?" he countered.

She dropped her eyes. Stark felt an odd kind of tremble somewhere near his heart.

"I don't know how I'll ever be able to thank you," she said softly.

"Just be there the next time I need a good lawyer."

She gave James Stark a look he couldn't begin to fathom. "You can count on it," she said.